NEW
823

THE HAUNTED VALLEY

AND OTHER GHOST STORIES

Mary Williams

Chivers Press • Thorndike Press
Bath, England   Thorndike, Maine USA

This Large Print edition is published by Chivers Press, England, and by Thorndike Press, USA.

Published in 1997 in the U.K. by arrangement with the author's agent.

Published in 1997 in the U.S. by arrangement with Laurence Pollinger, Ltd.

U.K. Hardcover ISBN 0–7451–8970–9 (Chivers Large Print)
U.S. Softcover   ISBN 0–7862–1042–7 (General Series Edition)

The text of this Large Print edition is unabridged.
Other aspects of the book may vary from the original edition.

Set in 16pt. Times New Roman.

Printed in Great Britain on acid-free paper.

British Library Cataloguing in Publication Data available

Library of Congress Cataloging-in-Publication Data

Williams, Mary, 1903–
 The haunted valley and other ghost stories / Mary Williams.
 p. cm.
 ISBN 0–7862–1042–7 (lg. print : sc)
 1. Ghost stories, English. 2. Large type books. I. Title.
[PR6073.I4323H38 1997]
823′.914—dc21   96–53907

CONTENTS

CHAPTER ONE

CELEBRATION

Miss Twigg and Miss Potter had lived together for so many years in their archaic house overlooking the village of Treesbrook they had become accepted by the inhabitants as an almost indigenous part of the countryside. The house was remote, ugly, of early Victorian period, fantastically intermingled with ornate balustrades and towers having sham gargoyles, mostly Eastern in type, poking incongruously from every conceivable corner. An ugly conservatory jutted out at one side, on the other a miniature pagoda-like erection obviously inspired by William Chambers' larger and more gracious version at Kew.

The whole effect was a formidable jumble of East and West hobnobbing in the worst possible taste, which was perhaps not entirely surprising since Miss Twigg's father had been something important in India during the Raj hierarchy, and Miss Potter's the younger son of an impoverished lord.

Both were unmarried, with a limited private income that enabled them to put up a brave front to the world, with the help of an ancient male retainer, and a governess cart in which they took regular visits to the village shop for

1

provisions ... Miss Twigg one week, Miss Potter the next.

Miss Twigg was tall, pale, thin and angular. Miss Potter broad and short, with an intimidating air commanding unfailing respect despite her lack of physical charm. Both indeed, were regarded with a certain awe by the villagers. The men ... farmers, labourers, postmaster, schoolteacher, and even the doctor ... never failing to touch cap, forelock or hat as they passed, a gesture acknowledged by both ladies with a slight inclination of the head and occasional flicker of a smile.

They never entertained. The vicar himself, who'd served the community for thirty years, had long since learned not to intrude on their privacy; so no one knew exactly the state of The Grove's interior except the ancient retainer who in due course shuffled off his mortal coil and was quietly laid to rest in the churchyard. Which of the sisters looked after their old pony then, no one knew.

After this the aged friends settled gradually into a more solitary life than before. Milk was delivered from the nearest farm and deposited on their doorstep with butter, cheese, and eggs. Weekly visits to Treesbrook became fortnightly, undertaken only by Miss Twigg in their old governess cart. When asked timorously by Mrs Bull, who kept the small shop, if Miss Potter was quite well, she was told with some acerbity there was nothing wrong at all but a 'touch of arthritis' in a 'what-business-of-yours-is-it?' kind of voice.

So no one bothered to enquire again, although it was noted that Miss Twigg's one long dark coat which she had worn since anyone remembered, needed repairing at the hem, that her face grew thinner and paler as the weeks and months passed, and her long nose more prominently inclined towards her chin. Her high-crowned hat wore a crushed saddened air above her white curls. But the imperious manner remained aloof and intact. Miss Twigg still remained in command of all she surveyed.

Then, one cold autumn afternoon an astonishing thing happened. Mrs Bull was extremely surprised when Miss Twigg arrived at the shop to enquire whether it was possible for Herbert—Mrs Bull's husband—to bring back four dozen red roses from Brinstow the next day.

'I know your good man goes in on market days,' the lady said, with one of her rare gracious smiles. 'It *is* rather far for myself or my friend to venture in our carriage. And the buses are so infrequent. I have a five pound note here which should cover the expense. And of course I will naturally re-imburse him for any trouble entailed.'

'Of course, of course, Miss Twigg,' Mrs Bull said, quite flustered by the whole occasion. 'Red roses you say, ma'am?'

3

'*Red*. Yes. They *must* be red ... as befitting the occasion.' And for a moment the prim face almost softened. 'A celebration. A very intimate little coming together. It is the tradition in *our* family *always* to observe the conventions.'

For a moment the tall figure seemed to sway slightly, and Mrs Bull thought her complexion paled, in fact became quite grey. But then the light was fading, giving the whole of Miss Twigg's tall shape a grey quality that was a little disconcerting. Of course it was probably the coat, Mrs Bull decided practically. For years now the poor lady's attire had been losing any pretension to real black, becoming dimmer and dimmer as the months passed until you could almost imagine it was a sombre dark-greenish shade sometimes. It was really sad, and her being such a gentlewoman too. How much she had in the bank no one knew; only that neither of the ladies would accept their rightful pension. This, to Mrs Bull, was exceedingly irritating considering so many people grabbed what they could without even, in *her* opinion, having a moral right to it. But there it was. When these aristocrats got 'bees in their bonnets' nothing could change them. Pride they called it. In Mrs Bull's opinion it was sheer stupidity.

A moment or two following the brief conversation, and with the arrangement that Herbert Bull himself should deliver the flowers

4

by two-thirty the next day, Miss Twigg departed, ostensibly to her governess cart, though no sound of the pony's hooves clopping away penetrated the still evening.

Yet it was very quiet, and suddenly chilly, Mrs Bull decided. There'd be a fog later, one of those yellow cloying things that penetrated every chink between doors and windows. Not the kind of weather at all to think of celebrations. Still, red roses would certainly give a little colour to that ugly drab house on the hill. Ugh! it gave her the willies merely to pass by. As for *living* in it ... almost as bad as living in a tomb; well not tomb exactly. Mausoleum was the word. One of those great morbid erections famous people of the old days had to house their dead.

'Do you know, Herbert,' she said to her farmer husband after he'd agreed, rather grudgingly, to visit the florist's the next day, 'there was something a bit funny about Miss Twigg when she called. I can't for the life of me think what, except that she seemed ... odd somehow. Not like herself; and she looked ill. Kind of grey.'

'Hm. Seems to me she's been odd as long as we've known her,' he replied. 'Both of them mad as hatters if you ask me. And how *old* are they anyway? Must be into the nineties. You don't expect a youthful flush at that age.'

'True enough,' Mrs Bull agreed, thinking how incredibly active Miss Twigg was when

5

you considered she'd known Queen Victoria in that legendary lady's last years. Of course Miss Twigg could have been a child then; but the fact made her well on into the eighties anyway ... or even nineties. Yet at rare times she still strode stiff-backed to the village, when their faithful nag was indisposed. Dear dear! Mrs Bull's tongue clicked against her teeth; perhaps she was *walking* back to the Grove that evening. The thought mildly disturbed her. How sad if anything had happened to their beloved crock of a pony. This could very well account for the soundless way the good lady had departed, and for her 'wisht' appearance too.

However, with a celebration in view this could hardly be the case. So Mrs Bull put the unpleasant thought out of mind, shut the shop and went to her kitchen.

Next day which was dismal, overhung with mist turning to thin rain, the farmer went on his accustomed jaunt to Brinstow market, returning in his cart to Treesbrook, with the four dozen red roses ordered by Miss Twigg. Grumbling a little, because he was tired and needing a bit of a rest and snack before seeing to farm affairs again, he set off on foot with the flowers carefully shielded in tissue paper.

'Don't know why *I've* got to play messenger boy,' he said glumly. 'A right Charlie I shall look and no mistake if folk see me laden with bookays. Sam would've gone for me.'

6

'I know, I know dear,' his spouse said. 'But it's not likely anyone will, in this weather. And you know what those two ladies are for *appearance* ... if you get my meaning. Sam's a good worker; but uncouth. That would *never* do ... not for Miss Twigg. Besides she asked for *you*, Herbert.'

So Herbert, hunched into raincoat and wellingtons, proceeded on his way with an inward conviction the whole world, as far as the female sex was concerned, was cock-eyed and selfish into the bargain.

He was back at Treesbrook forty minutes later looking so cold and wan his spouse was genuinely concerned.

'Gracious, Herbert!' she said, 'Whatever's the matter? You look as though you'd seen a ghost.'

'Ah,' he agreed, flopping into a chair. 'And I feel like it.'

'What do you mean?'

'When I got there,' he said, 'it was as quiet and silent as the grave, and that's God's truth. Not a light anywhere, but a candle or something flickering from one window. A shuddery-looking sort of place, Polly, and no mistake. All dark towers and corners dripping with rain, and those nasty stone faces leering over the door. Lawks! I thought, some celebration. But then I got hold o' myself, and pulled the bell...' he paused swallowing, while Polly stared round-eyed with fearful

7

fascination. 'Yes, Herbert, yes, go on.'

'The sound was horrible,' he continued, 'like the clang of doom, nothing less; and in a couple of minutes *she* came...'

'Who? Miss Twigg?'

The farmer nodded. There was a pause before he went on, 'An' I've never seen her looking like *that* before, *never*. Or anyone else for that matter.'

'Why? How?'

'Pale and shivery, an' so thin, you could almost *see* through her. She was holding a candle, and that made it all worse somehow. You know how folk look with a flame flarin' 'neath their jaws... well, maybe you don't. But I tell you, that long waxy face with its dark eye-holes and long quivering nose just put the fear o' the devil into me, Polly, and afore she could thank me or say a word, I just shoved the roses at her and took to my heels.'

'You mean you didn't wish her good evening or a happy party, or anything at all, Herbert? Not a word?' Mrs Bull asked incredulously.

'Not so much as a sausage, Polly. And I'm never going back there again, not for all the tea in China,' her husband said firmly. 'There's something wrong.'

'Well, perhaps we should get the doctor or police to call there.'

'You leave things alone,' he told her. 'No use getting involved with a couple of mad women. Let things take their course, that's what I say.'

8

And that's exactly what they did.

For a few days nothing was heard of Miss Twigg and Miss Potter until the nearby farmer who delivered milk and provisions reported that goods had been left at the back door of The Grove for over a week.

When the authorities eventually penetrated the interior of the house, a wave of foul stagnant air rushed to greet them. Cobwebs flapped in their faces; the stone floor streamed with damp and mice droppings. With handkerchiefs to their noses the officer and constable made their way down the dank hall, looking into each room in turn. All were in a state of poverty-stricken neglect, only a few relics of former prosperity remaining to mingle with the dirt and decay. There were no carpets on the floors, merely one or two threadbare rugs. The walls, except for an ancient portrait of a bygone military gentleman, attired in all his archaic splendour were empty; what furniture there was long since given over to dry rot and worm.

In a room at the far end of the corridor the two ladies were found. Miss Twigg was seated upright in a carved mahogany chair, one rose on her lap, facing a square swathed bundle in a rocking chair. On the floor an ancient nag's muzzle protruded from a bundle of sacking and threadbare rug, teeth bared, eyes glazed and very very dead. Roses were scattered all over the bony lump, and on the lap of the other

9

... the huddled female form, or what once had been female. Only Miss Twigg resembled anything that could be called decently human.

The mystery of course was how the roses ever came to be there. Though limp, they could have been present only a few days, and according to the pathologist, Miss Twigg had been dead at least a week.

As the Bulls didn't wish to be involved, no one heard the truth, and if they had would almost certainly not have accepted it. But since the macabre happenings, The Grove was left empty, at last to disintegrate into ruin.

However, on quiet nights still, when mist hugs the landscape into uniformity laying its grey shroud over fields and spectral building alike, some say horses' hooves can be heard through the silence ... others that a thin, tall, wraith-like shape sways momentarily on the hill-side before fading into the general gloom of earth and sky.

The truth?

Who can say, when fiction and reality so frequently meet and become mingled in the hinterland of the mysterious unknown.

CHAPTER TWO

FOUR'S COMPANY

The first thing that greeted me when I entered the house with my new wife Mandy was the heady sweet smell of Emma's bath salts. I had just placed Mandy on the mat after carrying her over the threshold, when the cloying scent drifted in a thick stream up the hall, almost knocking me backwards.

I put my hand over my mouth and nose and gulped ... at least I *think* I gulped, because Mandy said with that comforting concern in her voice natural to newly-weds, '*Darling!* what's the matter? You haven't caught cold, have you? Oh Peter, if you *have* it's *my* fault for having the window open. But the carriage seemed so stuffy...' her voice trailed off. She stared at me helplessly waiting for the denial.

I gave it.

'Nothing's wrong with me, sweet. It was just ... that smell. For a moment I thought...'

'*What* smell?'

Seeing with amazement that she really hadn't noticed it, I answered, 'Like bath salts. Really pungent. I've got an allergy to that sort of stuff.'

Mandy laughed. '*Bath* salts? The idea. Don't be silly, Peter. It's something left over from the

11

decorators I guess. Anyway...' with a shrewd gleam in her marvellous gold eyes '...I happen to enjoy my bubble baths in case you didn't know it. And that's *one* luxury I won't sacrifice, even for you, sweetheart. Another thing...'

'Yes?'

'There's no smell; nothing except a clean new house waiting to be loved and lived in.'

She was a bit off the mark there of course. The paintwork, decorative schemes, furniture, hangings, and carpets were new.

But the house wasn't.

Before she died it had been Emma's. And my first reaction when I smelt that insufferable perfume was that it was *still* hers.

Naturally it couldn't be.

It was mine.

She'd left me everything ... her whole half million including, as well, the house, Thorngates, which stood in ten acres of parkland, complete with stables and a studio where I could paint. So the bath salts business must have been a momentary association of ideas with the past.

I did my best to think so, and didn't find it too difficult during the first week with Mandy, who was so physically exuberant and absorbing...so bubbling over with energy and fresh ideas for adding to the decor, installing labour saving appliances here and there, and modern artistic touches meant to serve, I guessed, more as a background for her

12

individual type of beauty, than as cultural stimulus.

Mandy had no pretensions to tastefulness or conventional standards of any kind, which was one of the reasons I suppose, I had fallen for her so completely following the fiasco of marriage to Emma. Emma, the silly little thing, despite the blonde baby looks, assumed pout of rose-bud lips, gorgeous black-lashed blue eyes, proved to be a bore and a virgin at heart, entranced by clichés of 'love everlasting', 'this is forever', 'you darling sweet honey-bun', and oh! so many of them, and not one meaning a darn thing really, except to evoke, somehow, through sheer persistence answering responses from me.

There'd been times, many of them, when I'd wanted to put Emma over my knee and slap her hard. Perhaps it would have been better, and have saved a lot that happened later. But with Emma one simply didn't do such things. Everything had to be so sugar sweet and 'bee-ootiful', and restrained. It was amazing, when I thought back, that I'd been able to stand it for so long ... especially with her holding the purse strings in her firm little white hand.

Now with Mandy everything was just the opposite.

I'd no illusion about her past, which had been, she'd admitted, a bit lurid in parts. Well, I could accept that, so long as she behaved when *I* was around. The point was she was *fun*.

13

We could fight or make love as we chose, have one hell of a row one moment, and the next a real passionate 'making-up' that left us gasping and breathless, and wanting nothing in the world but to lie there together in the aftermath of consummation.

Mandy's body was a revelation; exciting, enticing, far more luscious than you'd have thought, seeing her in her smart trendy clothes. In fact I guessed she could easily become—in time—over-plump, to put it politely, if she didn't curb her physical appetites a little.

Once I put it to her. She laughed, shaking her long black hair from her breasts and said, 'Who cares? And don't be so pi. Say "fat", darling, and be done with it. Of course I'll be fat. What's wrong with that? My kind usually are.'

'And what *is* your kind?' I asked, with my pulses hammering.

She laughed, showing a tip of one tooth between lips juicy as red berries, got up, and jumping from the bed naked, rushed out of the bedroom with a flash of white flanks and buttocks, calling, 'Come and see, darling. Catch me ... if you can.'

This happened more than once, with Mandy running naked from room to room, down corridors and halls, upstairs and down again, until she'd had enough and was ready for what she'd hankered for at the very beginning— submission.

14

Oh yes. Life was hilarious, heady, and rewarding ... at the beginning. But of course going on as we did, we shied from any servants in the house, except a daily who came for mornings only. There was comparative quietness in the house then. Mandy was an adept at being able to present ... for a few hours anyway, the necessary front to suit a particular situation, and when Annie was around no one would have dreamed that she was other than what she appeared to be—a typical well bred country madam running her household with the appropriate dignity expected of her position. I must say she did it well, too. Mandy, in tweeds, with her glossy hair smoothed back and her luscious curves cunningly restrained by belt and bra beneath her expensive twin-sets, would have fooled anyone who didn't know her. And up to a point I thought she enjoyed playing the role for limited periods.

I didn't though.

It was at those times, when she was giving orders in the kitchen or busy about her shopping list, with a certain aloof note in her voice and wearing a toffee-nosed expression that commanded deference from lesser mortals such as Annie, the part time gardener, Binns, and I must admit, myself, that Emma's bath salts started their games again with my imagination.

Oh yes. It *had* to be imagination. What else

could it be? But it was frequently so strong I couldn't help exclaiming one day ... or rather exploding ... 'That ... that *stink*! What is it?'

Mandy, who was arranging some chrysanthemums in a bowl, turned sharply and replied, 'What do you mean ... *stink*? A horrible word. I *love* chrysanthemums if you must know. And their smell's invigorating; so earthy.'

'I wasn't talking about chrysanthemums,' I said shortly.

'Then what?'

'A ... a sweet smell,' I told her tactlessly. 'Like bath salts.'

Mandy sighed, remarking in a stately bored voice. 'Please don't start that lark, darling. *Bath* salts. It's a phobia with you, isn't it? I wish you'd told me. I've an aversion to neurotics. And if you mention that word again I'll bloody well walk out and not come back. Understand?'

The way she said that made me, for the first time, want to hit her, but I didn't. I controlled myself sufficiently to remark, 'And *that's* hardly a ladylike way to talk. When I say I smell something, I *do*. Perhaps you suffer from some allergy that makes you...'

'Smell-blind?' The simile was so ridiculous Mandy broke into a fit of laughter in which, after a moment, I too joined. That was her charm I suppose, partly, the way she could so quickly change from one mood to another.

16

Well, for a little while after that no subtle reminder of Emma materialised to break our mutual joy in each other.

It was autumn then, with the oaks and beeches in our garden turning to burning russets and rich molten gold, and with always the heady creeping odours of wood-smoke, fallen leaves and tumbled blackberries drifting from the woods and hills, across the lawn to the house.

Apart from shopping expeditions to Connisham five miles away and occasional evenings out at a restaurant, Mandy and I lived a quiet life cut off from social impact. We liked it that way, especially when lunch was over and the gardener gone for the day, leaving my wife and I free for our amorous indulgences.

She really could be outrageous then. One afternoon when I was trying to get a bit of paper work done in the library, she appeared at the door wearing nothing but a yellow flower behind one ear. Not a stitch on her anywhere.

The result of course was inevitable.

As I've said, it was mostly fun.

But one night following an arduous day I was woken from a heavy sleep by Mandy prodding me, with a hair-pin.

'What the ...?'

I sat up abruptly to see her standing by the bed, full in a beam of moonlight from the parted curtains, like some seductive plump nymph, with an odd luminous look about her

17

that somehow affronted me.

'What's the matter?' I asked querulously. 'Are you mad or what? Giving me a shock like that. Enough to...'

She flung herself on me. 'Smell me ... smell me...' She muttered with her face and hair against my cheek while I struggled to free myself. 'Isn't it nice? A brand new talc. "Incandescent" they call it ... because it's shiny and glows...' and she giggled.

'Get away,' I shrieked with sudden uncontrollable rage. 'Go on, get off. It's horrible and you should be ashamed. Go on, wash yourself and get something on before I...'

'Seduce me? But *darling*. It's too late for that, remember? And with such a *lo-o-vely* moon. Can't we ...?'

She stopped suddenly as she saw my face.

'*Peter*. What's the matter?'

To my shame I realised I was trembling. Not because of Mandy's sexual stupidity, but because of the perfume ... *Emma's*.

'Will you please do as I say, Mandy,' I told her more quietly. 'Go and freshen yourself with clean soap and water. I do *not* like the smell of that stuff. And it makes you appear...'

'What?' Her voice had changed, was cold.

'Cheap,' I answered uncompromisingly.

Her eyes glowed as her chin came out in the stubborn way it had when she was in a temper.

18

'Certainly. But don't expect me to come within an inch of you until you apologise, and *beg*.'

I didn't, and had no intention of doing either of those things anyway. Knowing Mandy, or *thinking* I did pretty well by then, I guessed she wouldn't hold out longer than a day or two at the most.

The trouble was, I hadn't counted on Emma.

The next morning I fetched Mandy's 'Incandescent' and took it to the waste-bin. Before I threw it away I had one sniff and got a surprise. It didn't smell like Emma's perfume *at all*; which was really odd, as the previous evening the whole room had reeked of it.

After that things got worse.

For the next two days during an icy estrangement in which only 'yes's' or 'no's' or 'hand-me-the-salt' sort of remarks passed between us, nasty sneaking little reminders of Emma seemed to be lurking everywhere, ready at the first opportunity to materialise at unexpected moments, and not only as perfumes any more.

For instance there was the *daisy* episode. Now in autumn one doesn't *expect* to see a bunch of those anaemic looking little flowers, freshly picked, lying on the hall table. And when I noticed them I didn't at first believe my own eyes.

Daisies! Emma's flowers. They'd been her favourite.

19

'So *sweet* and prim and pretty, the tiny things,' she'd said more than once in her 'little girly' kind of voice, 'I do like wild flowers, especially the weeny ones.'

The memory was so swift and clear, I jumped, half expecting to see her peeping over my shoulder. But there was no one except Mandy coming towards me from the foot of the stairs looking extremely handsome, condemning, and more than a little majestic in a well cut rather tightly fitting tweed skirt and orange sweater.

Not meaning to, I broke the silence by exclaiming irrationally, 'Did *you* do that?'

'*What?*'

'Those flowers. Those daisies.'

I looked round, pointing. They were still there, but paler somehow, less formed as though they were fading.

Mandy's voice held a pitying note when she said, 'I can't see any flowers. And daisies of *all* things. How *ridiculous*.'

Her contempt was so flagrant I caught her by the forearm with my fingers biting into her flesh, saying roughly, 'Look here, Mandy, I'm fed up with it, do you hear? If there's any more of this stupid business between us, I'll ... I'll ... I'll damn well ...'

'Beat me?' From chill derision her manner was changing to warmth and desire.

'Probably,' I answered, releasing her, but with my pulses hammering.

She burst out laughing. 'Oh *darling*! But how *absurd*! As if I'd *mind*. My sort of woman knows how to deal with a bit of horse-play. And anyway...' speculatively, 'I'm probably a good deal tougher than you think. So look out, sweet. You might get a nasty surprise.'

She turned her back on me deliberately, her stance and figure just inviting trouble.

But I didn't respond.

Instead, glancing down inadvertently towards the table I noticed something that drove Mandy completely out of my mind.

Only a faint damp mark where the flowers had been.

I went forward automatically, touching the oak surface with my finger tips, muttering to myself, 'They're gone. The daisies have gone.'

And at that moment a stronger-than-usual waft of Emma's foam-bath puffed into my face cloying my nostrils and throat so that my chest heaved in one tremendous sneeze. I took a handkerchief from my pocket, as Mandy said coolly, 'Ah. That explains it. You've got a temperature or something. Thank God.'

'What do you mean "thank God"?' I retorted, rubbing the tears from my eyes and nose.

'That you're not necessarily potty,' my wife told me complacently. 'All that blurb about daisies ... well! I *ask* you. But if you've a fever it's not so bad. I mean it shows you should be in bed, doesn't it? Come on now. Where's that

21

thermometer?'

'We just don't happen to have one, if you remember,' I told her acidly. 'When I mentioned having a medicine cupboard you pooh-poohed the idea, and that was that. Anyway, I haven't a temperature.'

'Sorry. I don't agree,' Mandy insisted, with the peremptory maddening bossiness of any hospital nurse. 'Bed's for you, darling, so don't argue.'

I didn't.

I just complied with her command like any infatuated schoolboy and got between the sheets knowing it was what she wanted, and that there'd be no peace until I did, realising as well that it was probably the lesser of two evils, since a bunch of etheric daisies would hardly have the physical stamina to mount a flight of stairs, whereas Mandy certainly *would* ... *and* me, into the bargain.

Which is exactly what happened.

Now I don't want to disparage Mandy. As I've already said, she was fun, great fun, without any of the inhibitions or phoney reserves that had made life with Emma so unrewarding. But as the days went by, there *were* times, when I realised the truth of the old adage, that 'you could have too much of a good thing' ... on occasion of course.

The fact was, her positive exuberance began to wear me down, and when this happened, Emma's bath salts intruded more frequently

22

upon our marriage.

If Mandy could have accepted the fact, admitted the ghostly odour, I'd have felt better, and probably have suggested we sold the house and moved somewhere else. The snag was she didn't, simply because she was impervious to the nasty stuff.

For her it didn't exist.

There were other things too.

Mandy's unfortunate habit of 'humming' about the place with a travesty of mostly *one* song ... a sentimental 'pop' item that had been Emma's favourite, 'Love, love, love in the air'. In Emma's lifetime it had been bad enough, but with Mandy it was worse, because her voice was throaty and harsh, setting my teeth on edge.

Naturally I tried to curb my irritation, but at times it was impossible. 'Can't you stop forever warbling that thing?' I'd shout, or something like it. 'It's a rotten tune anyway, and sheer murder the way you carry on.'

She'd be furious of course. Once she even tore downstairs in her underwear and clawed a chunk of my hair out. I did what I'd wanted to for some time then ... put her over my knee and walloped her soundly. Following that there was peace for a bit until Mandy's boredom overcame her hostility, and we were once more savouring the delights of reconciliation.

And then, gradually, Emma started up

again; or rather Emma's tricks.

Daisies once more appeared ... on the dining room table this time, in a small glass container ... where they hadn't been a moment before. Mandy was upstairs tidying her wardrobe as it was a grey day filled with thin drizzle, so I didn't hesitate but rushed to the window facing the lawn, then back and out of the front door just to prove whether *what* I'd seen out there—Emma or Emma's spirit wearing a white billowy flimsy thing—was true or false.

I rather guessed she'd be gone when I got there, and in a way I was relieved to find she had. But I was so scared the sweat was running as thick as the rain down my face; and so shocked I found myself saying, 'Stop it Emma. Leave me alone can't you? ... Emma ... Emma...' I looked round helplessly, peering through the fogged bare branches of the trees and huddled bushes, then down at the wet grass.

There was nothing.

No sign of footprints or a silly-ghost-face peering, and not a daisy anywhere. Just dripping desolation and a lurching fear at the pit of my stomach.

I turned and went back quickly to the house.

Mandy was waiting for me in the hall, wearing one of those multi-coloured Indian kaftan things that suited her so well.

'What are you up to?' she demanded. 'What

24

the heck's come over you, Peter? Just now when I looked down from the bedroom, there you were, standing all gooey-eyed, as if ... as if ...'

'Yes?' I prompted her because there seemed nothing else to say.

She shrugged and turned away. 'You know what? You're beginning to bore me to death, and that's God's truth. Here...'

She came back, taking a packet of cigarettes from her pocket, exotic Turkish things I didn't like. 'Have a smoke, and tell me about it.'

I waved her hand away.

'Thanks. I don't care for those things, Mandy. And there's nothing to tell.'

'No?'

'No. Except in the first place I wasn't gooey-eyed as you call it, and if I had been you couldn't possibly have seen. In the second...' I paused, before adding recklessly, 'there were daisies again, on the dining room table.'

'*Daisies?*'

'I've said so. *You* didn't put them there by any chance?'

'For *Heaven's* sake. Why *should* I? Don't be absurd.'

I believed her, because that sort of trick wasn't her line anyway; there was nothing in the least spiteful about Mandy.

'Come with me then,' I said, 'and have a look for yourself. With luck they may still be there.'

But they weren't.

25

When we entered the room there was nothing on the table at all but the small glass vase, quite empty, and my reading glasses. Naturally this evoked further derision from Mandy.

'You must be sick,' she said contemptuously. 'You should see a doctor.'

'*I'll* show you how sick I am,' I retorted, going towards her deliberately. But the sneer on her face checked any impulse I'd had with temporary cold dislike.

'Don't goad me, Mandy,' I said flatly. 'And don't play games. It's my belief *you* took those flowers away.'

'Me?' Her eyes widened. 'Why should I?'

'To get me locked up, put away perhaps?' I suggested spitefully. 'That would be quite an achievement on your part wouldn't it? To have everything under your grasping palm just like ... like Emma?'

There was a pause before Mandy exclaimed, obviously shocked, 'What a perfectly *foul* thing to say. I thought even *you* were beyond such ... such rottenness.' Her eyes were flaming in her face, which was wide at the cheek bones narrowing to a stubborn small chin with the suggestion of a second one in embryo, giving her a curious feline look. In middle age maybe, she *would* become stout, as she'd suggested, epitomising the image of a sexy cat-eyed matron too lazy to care for her figure but always sharp with her claws and tongue.

26

At that moment I didn't like her a bit. And she knew it.

When I didn't say anything, or offer the apology she'd wanted, she shrugged and walked away, retorting, 'You should watch your words, darling. I might take you up on your suggestion.'

Well, with interludes like this intruding more frequently upon our existence, the harmony of our married life was naturally impaired. Words of a certain kind once said, can be forgiven but never entirely erased. And though passionate interludes were always eventually resumed between us, doubt of Mandy's intentions was so secretly sewn in my mind by then, I started to watch her. Supposing I thought ... just *supposing* it was true and she really *did* want me out of the way. If it happened she'd be a rich woman on *my* money, the worry that had been Emma's. And she liked men, oh yes ... Mandy had never professed to celibate instincts. We had a very good looking postman at that time, and I'd noticed more than once the way she kept him at the door chatting, head slightly to one side, hand on hips, laughing ... I knew she was laughing by the way she tossed her hair back; the tip of her tongue would be showing cherry red between her teeth, her golden eyes gleaming. I'd want to beat the living daylights out of her then, but instead would go ineffectively for the cat, a long haired

27

vindictive ginger that had been Emma's and was forever leering at me, just out of reach.

I wouldn't have hurt the thing of course. In a general way I like all animals, including cats; but this one unnerved me simply because I'd a shrewd idea it sensed all there was to know about Mandy and me, and got a tremendous catty-kick out of it.

Or was Emma prompting him?

I'd learned by then to accept Emma's presence without question, etherically, that is. My main problem was not to let Mandy know.

And it became a strain.

There were even moments, as winter approached, when I'd see Emma quite clearly, a little mistily perhaps, but there all the same, watching me from the lawn, or even waiting at the end of the hall by the kitchen. But Mandy never did. In fact once or twice they both walked through each other, and I'd stand there speechless, with the stench of Emma's bath foam in my nostrils, wondering how long things could continue in that way.

The idea of going to see a doctor occurred to me, but I put it aside because of the inevitable mental digging and probing it would incur. I guessed what the verdict would be when I confided my 'hallucinations' as rational theorising would consider them. 'Over-tiredness'; 'neurosis' induced by 'emotional conflict', or worst of all ... some obscure 'guilt complex' from the past.

And I didn't want that. Sheer poppycock of course, but Emma's death *had* had its macabre side, and although I hadn't been involved, I easily *could* have been if I'd gone to her rescue a moment or two earlier, and found her still alive. Could I have resisted a final push? I doubt it. Morally I suppose I should have stopped her having her bath with no one about. She'd sprained her ankle earlier that day, and it was quite swollen. I'd warned her to be careful though, and anyway she was such a puritan about her lily-white little body, not being seen naked, even by me, the thought of violating her sensibilities had become obnoxious to me by then. I'd tried in the past to get a glimpse of her floating about all gooey-eyed in that foamy stuff. But even the sight of just her chin sticking above the bubbles, had caused such a furore she'd screamed and cried, 'Don't ... don't. Go away *Pet*ah'—she always said my name, like that,—*Pet*ah!—you shouldn't *pry*. It's not nice.'

'*Nice*!' I'd thought turning and slamming the door on her. What a joke. A bit of downright nastiness was what Emma needed. Cave-man stuff. But I was becoming too bored to give it. So when she'd screamed on that evening of her death, I'd taken no notice at first. Just a thud and a yell it was, and then silence. I was in the bedroom at the time, and I suppose any chivalrous male would have gone to her rescue at once, knowing about the ankle and how she

29

would run the water to the highest level of the bath. I wasn't chivalrous any more though. Emma's chill 'virginity' combined with her surprisingly tight little fist on the purse strings had effectively quelled any tender feelings towards her. 'Let her wallow in her own pain for a bit,' I'd thought. 'Serve her right.'

And when at last I'd got to the bathroom she was dead, lying face down in a steaming mass of foam. I'd lifted her head, and the sight of her face had made me drop it again, quickly. I'd pulled the plug out of the water, naturally, but hadn't tried to revive her. Why should I? The servants were out that day, so no one would know if I'd been in or not, and anyway it was best the doctor should see her first. On second thoughts I did trickle a little brandy into her gaping mouth, but as I'd expected, quite ineffectively.

Of course there were questions. But because what I told the Coroner was true: I'd heard her scream, gone to her rescue, and found there was nothing I could do but what I had; my word had been accepted and a verdict of accidental death recorded—with the rider that artificial respiration would have been better then the immediate administration of spirits in such an emergency, which proved the advisability of everyone learning the rudiments of first aid.

Relief had filled me at this satisfactory conclusion and freedom from marital

30

bondage. For six months I'd had a whale of a time digging into my late wife's tidy little fortune, enjoying bachelordom and women when I felt like it, without any strings attached.

Then, suddenly, wham! out of the blue had come Mandy, curse her.

Yes, it's no exaggeration to say that as the months went by I did, on occasion, curse both her, and myself, for having been ensnared again into matrimony. At other moments when she stood naked with her marvellous back to me, preening herself before the bedroom mirror, the sight of her slim waist flowing so seductively to full buttocks and plump thighs aroused the old primitive feeling in me, and I'd forget everything ... even Emma ... except the overwhelming need to assert my male and rightful prerogative, of possession.

It was generally after such sexual sessions that the Emma business started up again, destroying Mandy's newly retrieved joie-de-vivre and respect for me, and my own self-pride.

By January life was pretty intolerable; things of mine, small possessions, were constantly disappearing from where I'd put them, and popping up eventually in most unexpected places, under a cushion or on top of the bookshelves, in the kitchen, even the fridge, which was quite senseless, especially when the missing article happened to be a pipe. Guessing Emma was at the back of it, but unable to voice my fears to Mandy, I'd accuse her of playing about with things.

She'd flare up then saying I was either going out of my mind, or it was the cat.

'Look at it!' she sneered once, 'It's a beastly creature if ever there was one. Why don't you get rid of it?'

'Why should I?' I shouted back. 'You're not suggesting I hope, that *Leo* opened the fridge door and put my pipe there?'

'If Leo didn't, *you* did,' Mandy said nastily. 'Choose which one you like. If I were you I'd go for the cat.' And she flounced out of the room with that certain swing of her behind that made me always want to beat her. I contained myself though, and gave a long contemplative look at Leo.

He was seated perfectly statically on the best sitting room chair, staring at me, not malignantly exactly, but with a cold triumphant look in his green-gold eyes that gave me the shivers.

I went out abruptly, walking down the hall sharply towards the library. And it was then, lurking in the shadows at the foot of the stairs, that I saw Emma. Quite clearly defined, but with a luminous look about her as though she was lit up inside rather like a dim bulb, one of those antique incandescent things of Victorian times. *Incandescent!* my heart lurched as a thickening wave of that hateful bath foam and talcum powder intensified through the air.

And Emma smiled.

How she contrived the effect I don't know, but that smile was so smug, so ... so absolutely baleful, I felt sick. And as I watched momentarily petrified, all I'd ever wanted when Emma lived emerged for me to see, pointed flower-like little buds of breasts, and taunting slim limbs with girlish thighs tapering to knees and slender ankles.

Oh, she made an intriguing ghost. But when at last I'd got courage enough to go towards her she suddenly vanished, and there was nothing any more but the shadows of the stairs where they merged at the base into all the other shadows of the dying afternoon light.

It was about that time that I first began to think of us as a foursome living in the house ... Mandy, Emma, Leo, and me.

I never really made up my mind whose side Leo was on ... mine or Mandy's. But he certainly had an affinity with Emma, because I couldn't help noticing that every time she started her little tricks Leo was somewhere about.

And as it happened he was in the last trick of all—if it *was* a trick.

One evening Mandy and I had a frightful row, in which inadvertently or wittingly, I don't know, she kicked the cat. Leo's scream was blood-curdling as he shot away to the kitchen, sufficiently so to silence us both, leaving a brief scared look on Mandy's face.

Then she said, '*You* did that.'

'I didn't', I told her coldly, but breathing heavily. '*You* did ... you insufferable cold-blooded bitch.'

Now I know no man should talk to his wife like that; and after a few minutes I was about to make a belated apology when I heard it ... a low faint chuckle of glee. A silly sort of ghostly giggle.

Emma's.

I stood stock still waiting for her to appear; but she didn't. Probably I must have shown my fear, because Mandy remarked maliciously, 'Seen a ghost? Good. It's what you deserve, you ... you insufferable loud-mouthed bore, and I hope it chokes you.'

With which parting shot she took off upstairs, and locked herself in the bathroom. I didn't know how she *could* with that beastly odour seeping along the landing and downstairs. Then I remembered. With Mandy, Emma's bath foam just didn't register.

Well, the next few days were practically non-speaking periods for Mandy and me. The curious thing was that she and Leo became so matey ... practically inseparable, which was surprising considering the kick she'd given him. Whenever Mandy crossed my path, in her characteristic hip-swinging way, nose in air, chin up, Leo was generally following, waiting to twine himself round her luscious legs at the first opportunity.

It was really quite revolting; especially when she bent down saying in a throaty soppy way, 'Is he friends then? I really think he is...' or something to that effect, letting her full lips touch his damp nose. Once or twice I found him squirming on his back, legs in the air, with Mandy crouched down tickling his furry front. 'Nice fat tum-tum,' I heard her murmuring sickeningly. 'Lo ... ovely ... lo ... ovely Leo.'

And when I passed with an intentional thrust of my foot at both of them, she looked up with hate in her eyes. It was after such incidents that Emma began to materialise more firmly. At times, too, she'd even start to talk ... or rather whisper ... when there was no one about. Inane remarks naturally, as they were Emma's; brief coos and murmurs of ... 'Never mind *Pe*-tah ... everything will be gorg*ee*ous. You see ... you see ... Leo knows...' and the creakings and soughings of the old house in the winter wind would catch up and echo the last word, in a wave of etheric sighing, 'knows ... knows ... knows...' as the vision of Emma slowly faded and disintegrated in a cloudy mass of vaporous foam.

When I'd recovered I'd rush away, switch on all the lights I could find, even if it was daylight, or busy myself with violent activity like hacking logs for the fire. Often I'd turn on television and radio at the same time so the blare of sound kept other sounds out; and by then I didn't care what Mandy thought. I knew. She considered me a raving lunatic; her eyes said so, the curl of her lips, and sometimes ... just occasionally, a really scared look on her face. I was pleased by that. Scaring Mandy was quite an achievement. Only of course I knew there'd have to be limits or she'd contact the authorities ... whoever they were ... and manage by hook or crook to have me put away.

So I was wary.

As things turned out I needn't have been. I could have indulged myself a little more putting the fear of God—or the devil—into my sarcastic domineering spouse. The conclusion of our ill-starred marriage was inevitable, which I realised looking back.

One cold afternoon following a more than usual unpleasant scene with my wife, one in which I noticed Emma's half-formed visage peeping slyly from a corner of the bedroom, Mandy flounced out and down the stairs, slamming the side door behind her with a rattle that told me she was hell-bent on business this time, fetching a doctor probably, or perhaps even the police, because I *had* gone further than usual; and Mandy certainly wouldn't spare the punches. From the window I saw she wasn't wearing a coat, and looked what she was—a slut in disarray who'd got what she'd asked for. Leo was following though with the proud upheld furry stance of his tail triumphantly waving in the wind.

I was still trembling with rage and a dull

sense of fear as I saw them turn a corner of the path leading to the garage. I guessed where they were going, and found I was right when a minute later the car purred up the drive, and turned through the front gates, not wisely, but far too savagely for safety.

Still Mandy was a good driver, and with luck would probably get to the station in reasonable shape, I told myself logically.

But what about me?

I was going to be in a pretty hole when she arrived back accompanied by a couple of sturdy constables, and for the first time clearly realised my predicament. So I attended first to the main essentials that could possibly disprove her story ... tidied the bedroom, washed, changed from my casual weatherworn sweater and slacks into an expensive grey Savile Row suit, smoothed my ruffled hair into sleek submission, and when I'd satisfied myself I was actually one up in appearance on a middle-aged Cary Grant, sauntered downstairs into the library to await developments.

I had to wait precisely forty five minutes before the police, an officer and constable, arrived. And when I met them at the front door their attitude was positively deferential, with that particular half fearful look of commiseration on their sturdy faces that told me something had happened. Something very serious indeed.

37

It had.

Mandy apparently, on the outskirts of the town, had bumped into a telegraph pole, crashed the car to bits, and killed herself.

'We're extremely sorry, sir,' the older man said. 'It must be a great shock, but...'

'Yes, yes,' I agreed, feigning faintness. 'If you'll excuse me ... please go in...' indicating the sitting room. 'I'll ... I think I'll...' I stumbled through first and poured myself a stiff brandy. Then, when I'd apparently recovered, I asked, 'How did it happen exactly? Was she ... had she been drinking?'

'Oh no indeed, sir,' the officer replied, 'Nothing of that sort at all. As far as we can judge at present, the trouble was the cat.'

My pulses started to hammer. 'You mean *Leo*? A large ginger ... *our* cat?'

'Yes, sir. I'm afraid so. It was lying across her throat. And the obvious conclusion at the moment seems to be that it jumped up suddenly and caused her to swerve.'

'Oh. I see.' And suddenly I did.

'As you know, it was ... *is* ... a very *large* animal, sir, and not really the kind to take about in any car unless it's fully under control. We had quite a tussle to get it away. Claw marks all over the poor woman's neck.'

'Is the cat all right then?' I asked automatically.

'Oh, yes. Not a scratch on it. As a matter of fact we've got it with us outside, in a basket. If you don't want it sir ... under the circumstances...'

'Of course I do,' I said automatically, knowing that whatever they did with it, or wherever they took it, Leo would be with me, just like Emma was, forever. 'Yes, bring him in please. He was my wife's pet.'

That last remark added I'm sure just the right touch of sentiment under the circumstances, and was perfectly true, although they were not to know that the wife in question was Emma and not Mandy.

Identifying Mandy later was not pleasant. In fact if it hadn't been for certain personal possessions and the chunky jewellery she wore, I doubt if I'd honestly have been able to do it.

I was thankful to get away from the mortuary, and home again, even though, as I entered the hall, that old sickening wave of Emma's bath foam rose to greet me.

Leo was obscenely pleased with himself, purring wildly, with a deep undertone, as Emma's voice whispered in my ear, 'Peace at last, darling ... just you, and me, and Leo.'

But she was a bit off the mark there.

Peace? Maybe. If you can call living with ghosts peaceful. Yes, I have to admit there are two of them now ... Mandy and Emma, which makes four of us living in communion together. I wish I could add the word 'harmonious'.

But it wouldn't be true.

Leo himself seems satisfied. But me?

Well ... although there are no fights any more, and periods of comparative quiet reign over the household it is disconcerting to say the least to have Emma popping up one moment and Mandy the next. They don't whisper to each other, naturally. Only to me. And their favourite game seems to be hiding things, small personal possessions of mine which take up most of my time in finding again.

One moment there are flowers on the table. The next they have disappeared. Emma calls softly from the bedroom, but when I get there I see Mandy in all her blossoming ghostly 'altogether' as they put it.

Sometimes I catch a waft of bath foam and see a dim figure floating down the hall. But when I reach the spot it's only Leo.

Maybe I should move. The doctor says so. He has a nice bed ready for convalescence in a private home. But I refuse to go; it would be no good, and being harmless as I am, no one can make me.

So I've resigned myself to the inevitable and making the best of communal living as one of a strange foursome ... Emma, me, Mandy, and Leo.

And the happiest of all I think, is Leo.

CHAPTER THREE

THE HAUNTED VALLEY

You either love mountains or you don't. You have to follow their mysterious call or there's no call for you at all.

With me mountains have always been, and still are, a passion. In sleep I dream of them, and whenever circumstances permit, I'm away on my own, putting up at some remote country hostelry where I can ramble and climb alone among the peaks of our own great hills.

I suppose you could call it a fever. For some it's the sea ... those who are never content without the smell of salt and foam in their lungs. Myself ... it's for the tang of heather and fine rain on the face from lowering mountain skies.

When I think of death, which most men of my age do on occasion, it's with a secret prayer in me that I'll meet it on a mountain top ... somewhere in the Black Mountains of Wales perhaps, where the summits loom dark over the great bowls of shadowed valleys, or wreathed in thin clouds which can suddenly part revealing a vista of unearthly beauty.

I've stood many times there watching the mist roll away leaving the hills briefly tipped to gold, stretching faraway, as far as the eye could see. There'd be brightness for a moment holding all the colours of the universe; then suddenly it would be gone, taken into silvered grey.

Lonely it is there, yet so filled with splendour and brooding knowledge, my heart aches when I remember.

Yes. More than half my life is spent remembering now. Most of all remembering that one afternoon when I found the valley. I'd been climbing since one, and by three-thirty thin wild rain was falling soft against my face taking the dying sun into a radiance of shivering light.

The summit I reached was not high as mountains go, and where land met sky was a rounded lonely ridge of fine turf broken only by lumps of rock, and the distant forms of two mountain ponies racing with flying manes towards the Northern ridge. Below me were valleys . . . secret valleys of darkening shadows, crouched narrowly between the great hills. There was no sound anywhere, and no movement there but an occasional sheep moving slowly as a grey shape against the deeper greyness of the undulating landscape.

And then I saw the boy.

As the fine rain momentarily cleared, he appeared a little ahead of me, walking casually along a narrow track cutting abruptly down the opposite side of the hill.

He was carrying a thorn stick and wearing a

brown tunic. His black curls appeared tipped with gold, and when he turned his eyes startled me, they were so brilliant in his brown face, yet filled with a gentle knowledge far beyond his years.

Not more than twelve I'd say, possibly younger. But there was a mature majestic dignity about him, curiously compelling.

So I followed him silently ... he did not speak ... along the thread of path, winding downwards in a milky white thread to the valley below. And when I got there he disappeared into the wreathing landscape of light and shade and drifting mist which rose intermittently to a calm and glowing splendour of quietness.

For a moment or two I just stood there, knowing I had come upon something infinitely wonderful and beyond man's knowledge or understanding. Then I went on and as my sight grew accustomed to the fitful light I caught here and there the glimpse of a window or door carved in rock. There were people passing ... people with a proud look on them, who eyed me strangely and then went on. Their feet were soundless, and they never spoke. Yet I was aware all the time of life continuing, of beings about their ordinary work, a craftsman at his bench, a woman wearing an apron with a basket on her arm, and children with rose-dark wondering faces turned towards me. I wanted to touch one, and raised an arm, then desisted.

It was as though the whole terrain and its habitat was suspended in time ... caught in a moment of unearthly silence, of deep communion and content holding the quality of a million years.

It is hard to explain ... impossible to put into words that brief and wonderful revelation of timelessness. For an instant I wondered if I'd died, but when I moved my foot there was real earth beneath, and my nostrils were filled with the sweet tang of mountain turf and flowers.

I've no knowledge now how long I waited there, spell-bound in a place that was real yet somehow beyond my grasp.

But after a time I turned, forcing my steps up the milky track from where I'd come, and when I looked back the mist had thickened to a creamy veil, obscuring everything into silent negation.

* * *

Later, when I reached the hostelry, I told the landlord of my experience.

He flung me a shrewd, yet half-frightened look as he inquired, 'Is it telling me you are, you saw the *boy,* sir?' And his voice when he mentioned 'boy' was awed, almost non-believing.

I nodded. 'A boy in brown, carrying a thorn stick. I followed him into the valley.'

'You did, sir?'

'It was so quiet there,' I said, rather tritely. 'I've never known such quiet before.'

'Yes, sir. So it would be, sir,' he agreed.

'What's the name of it, that hamlet?' I asked. He shook his head.

'No one knows that. No one ever has sir. But they call it the "Hidden Valley". And they do say ... but this is the legend, sir ... that anyone who looks on it sees nothing any more just as it was before, nor wants to either.' There was a pause before he continued, 'Only to remember they say. Just to remember.'

And it has been that way with me ever since.

As I said at the beginning ... you either love mountains or you don't. You have to follow their mysterious call or there's no call at all.

Well, I heard the call, and I've never forgotten ... the mystery and the quiet, and the proud brown faces of the lordly ones who walk there. I've wanted nothing ever since but to find it again, and now I know I never shall in this life. I've searched and searched each mountain and valley of the remote mysterious area, but the one I want evades me.

I have never married or looked on any woman with desire. Worldly ambition has not concerned me.

One glimpse has been sufficient to last my days. Though of what? ... How can I say when every attempt to explain the unexplainable must necessarily fall so far short of the truth.

CHAPTER FOUR

DUTY

Martha Marriott disliked her half-sister Melissa, though Melissa, being young, and very much in love with her fiancé, a junior tutor at Camston Art School, never suspected it.

Melissa had all the attributes Martha did not possess ... charm, looks, and a friendly nature, whereas Martha was dour, heavy-faced, with a sharp tongue and domineering manner.

But she *did* have one thing denied to Melissa ... *money*; having inherited everything the late Silas Marriott possessed, which was a tidy fortune, including the ugly Victorian house, Four Towers, where the two sisters lived.

Put on paper the description *does* have a fairly-tale flavour about it, but then real life frequently has when seen in retrospect.

And the truth was that when Melissa insisted blithely on becoming engaged, Martha knew she had to do something about it.

Her dislike at that time was pretty well camouflaged—even to herself—by a sternly implanted sense of duty; and it was quite clear to her in this instance that she had to guard her sister from making the tragic mistake of marrying an impecunious fortune hunter!

She began by pointing out, she hoped

logically, that when anything happened to her, which would almost certainly be long before Melissa's demise as there was a whole eighteen years between them, Melissa would inherit.

'People know this,' she stated calmly, 'and you're bound to have ambitious young men with no conscience after you. So you really must be sensible and see things as they are, and not necessarily as you *want* them to be ... at the moment.'

Melissa laughed. 'Don't be such a fuddy-duddy, Martha. As if I wouldn't *know* whether Tristan loved me or not. You're such a *worry*, and all about the wrong things. You wait till we're married. One day you'll see I'm right.'

But Martha had no intention of 'waiting', and though she tried to conceal it, her dislike of Melissa—or perhaps of Melissa's happiness—from that moment turned to acute obsessive hatred. 'Fuddy-duddy' indeed! she thought with a tightening of her primped-up mouth, and *Tristan*! what a ridiculous name for any man. It just showed what type of parents he must have had. The trouble was of course that she had been weak in allowing Melissa to go to art classes at all. She'd refused point blank at first to supply the wherewithal, but when her young sister a few days later had hinted at joining some pop-group or other, Martha had abruptly changed her mind. *Pop*, the very idea! All long haired layabouts and drug-fiends—the possibility could not be tolerated. *Art* at least could bring beauty into life, if viewed from the right angle. It was ironic, she decided later, that all it seemed to have done so far was to sweep Melissa straight into the arms of a trendy young man with mercenary inclinations, and probably no morals at all.

All the same, following one or two quite exhausting arguments it became clear to her that subtler tactics were necessary, and under a front of grudging acquiescence she invited Tristan to Four Towers for an evening meal in the early autumn.

The sycamores and elms fringing the Midchester suburbs were by then turning greenish-yellow tinged with the first touch of orange. Leaves from the few chestnut trees at the frontage of the house already lay like dead hands on the faded grass, with just a few left hanging from the dark branches. It had been a hot summer, and nothing looked quite fresh any more, even the chrysanthemums in the borders of the garden had a tired appearance, while the ornate towers of the building loomed forbiddingly and stubbornly reminiscent of their period against the fading evening sky.

For Martha the setting was completely and harmoniously in key. She was a typical representative of stalwart respectability, with dark-fringed 'bobbed' hair, strong features, an inclination for wearing subdued shades of beige and brown ... especially sensible twin sets, that did nothing for her colourless complexion. Her figure was sturdily commanding, and on the evening in question clad in a severely cut black silk dress, of mid-calf length which unfortunately emphasised instead of diminished her spreading fortyish curves. At one shoulder was pinned a diamond brooch that had belonged to her mother . . . an incongruous but compelling symbol of her power and prestige in the household.

Melissa, to the contrary, appeared enchanting in a green flimsy maxi frock emphasising her dusky gold hair, creamy skin and amber slightly tilted eyes that at times seemed to catch all colours of earth and sky.

Tristan had told her this during their first romantic moments, and ever since Melissa had been aware of her appearance, something her sister was quick to notice and condemn.

'What's that material?' she'd demanded when Melissa had first worn the frock.

'Butter muslin. Dyed of course.' Melissa had replied with a hint of triumph. 'And don't tell me it's a waste of money. It's my own, isn't it? Oh Martha, do *smile*.'

Ignoring the appeal Martha had retorted sharply, 'From your allowance of course. What I give you for materials.'

Not wanting Martha to see the quick flush of humiliation, Melissa had turned away, saying. 'Unfortunately yes, Martha. But I've been economical with paints and things lately. And anyway, as soon as Tristan and I are married you'll be free of having to keep me, so it will be a good thing for all of us, won't it?'

'Tristan ... *Tristan*!' Martha had thought with a positive venom of rising fury. How dare the girl flaunt his name in her face like that. An upstart! ... a ... climbing parasite intent on destroying the habitual family routine of Four Towers.

It must *not* be allowed. It *would* not. She would see to it somehow, that the stupid engagement business was nipped in the bud and Melissa brought to heel.

It was her *duty*.

Duty remained the ideal she strived for; the indisputable weapon for moral attack, however tedious the effort might be.

And it *was* tedious.

Also extremely distasteful at that first meeting, having to smile and nod and agree to the subtleties of modern art, even while confessing not to understand it.

'I'm afraid I'm really rather a ... naive, shall we say ... person, in such spheres,' Martha remarked modestly as the three of them sipped coffee in the drawing room after an excellent dinner. 'I have not mixed much you see, in current cultural society, having had my time so well filled looking after Melissa ...'

The young man nodded with his fair-lashed, very clear, blue eyes speculatively on his hostess's face.

'Of course not,' he agreed, adding with a

51

smile which quite changed his appearance from that of a somewhat discomforting intellectual into that of a sunny-faced overgrown boy. 'Melissa's been lucky having such a good sister and fine home.'

Was there a hint of mockery in his voice? Martha was not sure, but she replied a shade more tartly, 'I am quite a bit older of course...' As if he didn't know, he thought with dry amusement; who in his senses could compare a gorgeous girl like Melissa with such a bulging battleaxe of a woman. Nevertheless he managed a polite '*Really?*' But no more.

'That's why I wanted to meet you, naturally. I feel responsible, and if I hadn't approved of your friendship with my sister, I...'

'Oh, Martha. Don't be so pompous,' Melissa interrupted, 'I'm not a child.' The angry red suffusing Martha's plump cheeks caused her to add in more conciliatory tones, 'I know you *think* I am. But I'm twenty-one; that's quite an age.'

'Not really,' Tristan said tactfully, if ambiguously, wanting peace restored. 'I'd say Miss Marriott was perfectly right. You *do* need looking after, and must have been quite a handful.'

Martha perceptibly relaxed.

'Oh well, we won't wrangle. It's up to us to be all three in harmony if possible. I do dislike arguments.'

Actually she had thrived on them all her life,

especially with Melissa; and a little of the zest had gone out of things when her half-sister, at last realising it, had relapsed into silence whenever controversy arose, instead of attempting to answer back.

'Answering back' had been a punishable offence in Melissa's childhood, and as Martha had always managed to be 'in the right' there'd been no point in attempting to prove otherwise.

But obviously, Martha thought that evening, Melissa's obnoxious 'young man' was fanning her rebellious instinct to life again. It simply would not do.

Arguing in private was one thing.

In public quite another

And the fact that there was something enigmatic, even contemptuous perhaps, about Tristan's manner, however soft soapy his words, only added fuel to the fire.

'He's decidedly a scrounger,' she told herself forcibly, while at the same time noting with grudging unconscious jealousy, the strong lithe limbs, firm sensuous lips above the neatly cut golden beard, and the soft gleam of his blue eyes every time he glanced fondly on Melissa.

To be kissed by him!

The mere thought of it brought a flush of shameful ardour to Martha's plump body so well corseted under the black dress.

What a horrid suggestion.

And to think that's what happened when

Melissa and Tristan were alone together. Kissing, and perhaps other things? Her own momentary sensuous aberration turned swiftly to renewed cold hate.

And that evening the first seeds of her plan were sewn. On the pretext of wishing to show Tristan some old photographs kept in a drawer of her chest upstairs, she conveniently despatched Melissa to find them.

'You may have to poke round a bit,' Martha said. 'If it's not in the chest I may have pushed the album into the boxroom cupboard somewhere. Have a good search, and bring it down. You know what it looks like, don't you ... covered in brown suede with a clasp ...'

Melissa's eyes were suspicious for a moment.

'Couldn't you ...?'

'Yes?'

'Oh well ... all right.' Defeated by that one clipped sharp word, Melissa, trying not to show her annoyance, went away grudgingly, leaving her sister and Tristan alone.

'*Now*,' Martha said as the echo of Melissa's footsteps finally died along the landing above, 'Come and sit by me on the sofa, or bring your chair up if you like. We must have a little chat.'

Her smile deceptively beguiling, took him momentarily off guard, although something about her ... her eyes, probably, which were small, very dark, and watchful, disturbed him. What they had to talk about he could not

54

imagine, unless it was his income which was far smaller than he wished.

However, when he'd drawn a little closer to her, he soon discovered to his great relief finance was not the problem.

'I'm quite a rich woman, in case you don't know it,' Martha said after a few formal preliminaries concerning his parents, background, and education had been successfully dealt with, 'and believe me my first concern will be, *always*, to see that Melissa has everything materially ... she's been used to in life. What I'm trying to say is ...' She paused, breathing heavily; a motion Tristan observed with some embarrassment, adding an extra life of its own to the rhythmic rising and falling of the black silk.

'Yes, Miss Marriott?'

'Well ...' she shrugged, 'I'm just trying to point out ... as tactfully as possible that if you ... *when* you marry my sister ... you will not have to worry unduly about your household expenditure. With her being as she is makes it more than ever necessary she should have no worry ...' her voice trailed off significantly. There was a brief awkward silence until Tristan said, 'I'm afraid I don't understand. Melissa's aware of what I earn, and she's prepared to make do on it. We both are. And ... what did you mean by "her being as she *is*"?'

'*Ah.*' Despite the worried frown on Martha's forehead, her voice was smug. Fatuous. Then she added with a sigh, 'You don't know of course.'

'What?'

'My dear boy ... excuse me, Tristan ... Melissa hasn't told you I suppose. Well, she couldn't exactly, as she doesn't know the full facts herself. You see ...'

'Yes?'

'Oh dear!' under a veneer of distress, Martha got up, walking a few paces to and fro, looking for all the world, Tristan thought, like a glossy, stout, disturbed pouter pigeon. Then she went to the window, stood there for a few moments as though considering her position, before returning to the couch, patting his hand gently and remarking, 'Have you not noticed that Melissa has *moods* sometimes?'

What on earth was the woman getting at, he wondered, as he answered ambiguously, 'Don't we all?'

'Yes, yes, of course. Up to a *point*. But, the truth is, and *please* don't let it come as too great a shock because most of the time she's *perfectly* all right. Through her mother though, there's always a *risk*, if you understand ...'

'I'm afraid I don't.'

'My father's second wife was not *normal*. She had periods of ... instability shall we say, that proved distressing to her family. It was not her fault, poor thing. There was a hereditary taint.'

So clipped, so completely without emotion

56

and so final, there was no mistaking her meaning, and when the truth registered, Tristan at first refused to accept the implications.

'Not Melissa,' he managed to say after a long drawn out pause. 'She's always been— seemed to me—the most natural, reasonable, and spontaneous girl in the world. I'm sorry, Miss Marriott, I don't want to hear any more, and I wish you'd not said anything. Her mother's health doesn't really concern me. All I care about is Melissa.'

'Of course. Of *course*. That's what I *mean*, what I'm trying to explain. So long as you give her all your love and care without any niggling worries to harass her, everything I'm sure can be perfect between you. Providing you don't have children of course.'

'But...'

'Unfortunately these mental disorders frequently crop up distressingly in a third generation. That's why I've tried, and generally succeeded up to now... in preventing Melissa from getting seriously involved with any young man. I realise now though, having met you and seen you together, that you are obviously *the* one. I shouldn't have said anything otherwise, but under the circumstances I had to. Don't you *see*, Tristan? It was my *duty*?'

With her chin poked forward very near to his, her small eyes peering intently at his face, he could only murmur, 'Yes, yes. I understand. But ...'

'But what?'

'Why didn't Melissa tell me herself?'

Martha looked aghast.

'My dear *boy*! I *told* you; she doesn't *know*. And she certainly mustn't ... not *ever*. If you said *one word*, gave the *slightest hint* of anything like that, it would be sufficient to send her completely ...' her voice wavered.

'Mad?'

'I didn't *say* so. Unbalanced sounds nicer. Since my stepmother's death when Melissa was only a baby, we've never mentioned the word mad, and I hope you'll remember it. Promise?'

He nodded dumbly.

'And I hope too, very much, that you'll be happy together, and that you'll manage to forget our sad little secret. As I said, I shall be as generous as possible with Melissa's marriage settlement. It means a great deal to me to know she's found someone as kind, as loving as you to look after her. So let us dismiss the subject once and for all. There should be no gloom to spoil an engagement party, which is what this is, isn't it?'

'Yes Miss Marriott ...' he found himself answering mechanically. 'We didn't exactly ... I mean ...'

'You didn't mean to give me the shock all at once!' Her brittle laugh trilled its jarring falsetto in his ears. He could feel her plump

58

hand patting his cheek lightly, but lingering for a fraction longer than was pleasant. With a sudden inner longing to escape, he glanced towards the door.

Martha noticed.

'What an impatient lover you are,' she mocked, trying to hide an irrational annoyance. 'Melissa's having to search, poor girl.' She laughed again, on a lower note this time, adding with subtle intimacy, 'I'm quite a scatterbrain sometimes, although I suppose it's hard to believe. But when I was Melissa's age ... ah!' she sighed reminiscently, 'I was considered quite wayward. My hair was so dark and so *long* ... far longer and thicker than Melissa's, and I was said to have a very good figure. It sounds ridiculous now, doesn't it?' Her manner had become rueful, almost coy.

Sensing what was expected of him, he replied gallantly, 'Not at all, Miss Marriott...'

'Martha,' she interrupted.

'Martha.' he replied. 'I'm sure you were ... still are ... quite handsome.'

'Not like Melissa though.'

This was too much for him, and he replied bluntly, '*No.*'

'I take after my *own* mother of course,' she said smugly but with significant implication. 'She was a Cave-Heron. All the Cave-Herons were dark,' and her shrewd eyes caught his with something more in them than mere desire to impart family history. 'Very white skinned

59

of course,' she added when no response was forthcoming. 'In fact when I was growing up ... before my dear father died he'd got into the rather ridiculous habit of calling me his "darling Mag". Not because my second name happens to be Margaret, but because my skin, he said, was pale and soft as a magnolia. Can you imagine *that*? ... A man ... and a *father* into the bargain ...?' As if to emphasise the point, she let her fingers stray to the neck of her dress above the tightly fitting bodice from where the flesh *did* emerge he noticed, surprisingly firm, white, and satin smooth. The observation startled him, and he was wondering how to reply, when mercifully there was the sound of a door slamming above, followed by hurried footsteps on the stairs.

Melissa burst into the drawing room a minute later, looking faintly flushed, with momentary suspicion in her lovely eyes.

'The album isn't *there*, Martha,' she said. 'You must have put it somewhere else...'

'My dear girl, I ... *oh*!' Martha's tongue clicked against her teeth. 'I'm so *sorry*. Of *course*, I remember now. What a scatterbrain I am—almost as bad as you, Melissa—I took it out only last week and put it safely in the secretaire in the library. *No*. no...' as Melissa moved impatiently to the door again. 'You have your little tête-à-tête with Tristan, and I'll get drinks for us at the same time ... it's the au pair's evening off you know,' she added, 'and

Mary, the maid, has gone to see her mother for an hour.'

'I don't think...' Tristan began, looking at his watch, but Martha waved her hand airily ... 'Now no excuses. Don't say you haven't time. Of *course* you have, on this occasion.'

She got up and strode across the carpet, moving, despite her well padded contours, with a certain sturdy grace that gave—for want of a better word—'oomph' to her firmly rounded buttocks, especially when the light caught them, satin black under the light.

When she'd gone, Melissa said contritely, with a placating troubled look in her eyes, 'Oh darling, I'm so sorry.'

Tristan patted her hand gently, kissed her temple, and then her lips, 'What for?' He remarked lightly, 'It's all right. Everything's okay so long as I've got you.'

Trying to believe him, and with her head resting against his shoulder, Melissa asked presently, 'What did you talk about?'

'Oh ... this and that. Small things. You, I suppose,' he answered. 'Mostly you.'

'What about me?'

'Well if you must know,' he told her, with forced banter, 'she's fallen for me completely, and thinks I'll make you *the* perfect husband of all time.'

'Did she say that?'

'Not precisely in those words. But that was the gist of it all right.'

61

He felt her body sag slightly against him in a sigh of relief.

'Do you really *mean* it?'

'Yes. It's true. Ask her if you don't believe me. Another thing, which of course being a mercenary character, pleases me no end ... she's sending you to the slaughter with a marriage dowry I can hardly wait to get my greedy fist on.'

'You liar,' she laughed.

'No. Honest injun. I told her we didn't want it ... at least I *think* I did ... but she insisted all the same. Your sister, darling, is quite a girl in her own way.'

'*Girl?*'

'Well ... *she'd* like to think so,' he said, recalling with momentary embarrassment the coy hot glance of the shrewd eyes, the white firm flesh so tightly encased in its near-bursting black sheath.

There was a pause before Melissa said slowly, 'I can't somehow ever imagine Martha being really young ... a girl, I mean.'

'Probably because she was nearly grown up when you were born.'

'Yes. With mother dying so young Martha took charge, except for the nurse and governess ... doesn't that sound stuffy? ... and when I went to school naturally they left, leaving just Martha, except for the servants.'

'I gathered something of the sort.'

'I suppose it was a bit restricting for her. I

62

was only eight when our father died, which meant she's always felt so *responsible*. I hate that. I always have; if only she wasn't so...'

'What?'

'Oh *faddy* in some ways. Old fashioned; *devoted* if you like. It makes it difficult in a way ... for *us* I mean.'

'I don't see why it should,' he said rather shortly.

She didn't reply at once and in the brief silence he felt the atmosphere converging upon him in a possessive unpleasant way which had nothing to do with Melissa, but was concentrated somehow in the lofty high ceilinged room, the Victorian furnishing, glass-fronted china cupboard, thick carpet, rugs, heavy velvet curtains, immense lustre chandelier, and wall lamps. Luxurious yet oppressive; the epitome of a period he detested, and yet now, it seemed, was going to be inevitably a portion—however small—of his life.

If he allowed it, that was. And damn it ... why *should* he? When he and Melissa were married he'd see to it no old bag of an elder sister came poking her nose in, trying to interfere. 'Old bag' though ... as soon as the term sprang to mind he had to dismiss it. There was nothing of the 'old bag' about Martha Marriott. Recalling the rhythmic predatory rotation of her buxom hips and thighs ... the dip of white flesh where firm breasts swelled

63

into the black shining bodice, he was revolted by his own instinctive sneaking sense of desire that the next moment had died again into chill dislike.

Then Melissa said quietly with a hint of anxiety in her voice, 'She's going to be lonely, you know.'

'I wouldn't worry about her if I were you,' Tristan said bluntly.

A moment later Martha entered with glasses and wines on a tray.

'What was that I heard about worry?' she queried lightly. 'I couldn't help hearing, you know.'

'Oh nothing, Martha,' Melissa answered with a deepening rose-glow in her cheeks. 'Nothing important. Only about small things...' she shrugged, 'just...' her voice trailed off.

'About me? You silly child. I've already told Tristan ... nobody could be more pleased than myself about your engagement. And there's nothing to worry about at *all. Nothing*, you understand! So stop fretting about a single thing. Everything's going to be *perfect.*'

But it wasn't.

Following that first visit to Four Towers, a faint but intangible shadow ... too frail at first to admit, crept insidiously into Tristan's mind, clouding what should have been one of the happiest periods of his relationship with Melissa.

It was not that he was less fond of her, or that her beauty and attractions for him had in any way diminished. Simply that at times, on rare occasions, Martha's warning, so carefully concealed under a show of care and thought for her sister, returned insidiously to taunt and torment him.

He was not sure that he believed it, mostly he didn't. But the suggestion still remained; a query he daren't put to Melissa for fear of shocking and hurting her, and as the days passed it troubled him more.

Martha suggested that they married shortly after Christmas, so they could begin their New Year together.

'Apart from the—dowry,' she said one day, with a puffed-up pleased look on her face as self-satisfied as any mother hen with a couple of chicks. 'I shall give you a house. Well ... a cottage really. I discovered it last week, a *dream* of a place, about five miles away from here, on the edge of the forest. I'm sure you'll love it ... no one in their senses could resist, and from what I know of Tristan ...' again the coy look in her small eyes, 'I know he'll absolutely agree ...'

After a speechless moment Melissa burst out, 'But *Martha*! D'you mean you've actually *bought* a place, without telling us? Without letting us see it first?'

'Of course dear. That's what I've just *said*. Now don't spoil my *surprise*. Oh Melissa, I

thought you'd be pleased. After all...'
critically, 'property is not cheap these days.
Most young couples in your position would
jump for joy at being spared the trouble and
expense of having to deal with mortgages or
loans and boring visits to a building society. I
do think you might be a bit grateful.'

'We *are*,' Tristan assured her promptly. 'It's
a ... a very generous gesture Miss Marriott,
and...'

'Martha,' she reminded him again.

'Martha. Yes, I must try to remember,' he
agreed with a touch of embarrassment.

He did his best to feel assured and pleased
about the cottage, and when, accompanied by
Melissa and Martha, he saw it later, there was
nothing he could have complained about, or
anyone else for that matter. Though
modernised and equipped with all labour-
saving devices, it still retained its original
Elizabethan character, including original oak
beams in the sitting room, inset stone fireplace,
where logs could be burned, plus cunningly
concealed wall-heating, and a large electric
fire.

The two bedrooms had whimsically slanted
ceilings under the freshly thatched roof, with
dormer windows intact, and a further large one
added to the west side.

Melissa was entranced, running from one
room to another, down the hall to the kitchen,
then upstairs again, exclaiming, 'It's lovely ...
lovely.'

Her cheeks were flushed, her eyes brilliantly happy.

'You see?' whispered Martha to Tristan meaningfully as Melissa disappeared momentarily to inspect the bathroom.

'What?'

'How ... how enthusiastic she is.'

'Well, naturally.'

'Yes. But I mean, just slightly excessive. Oh, I don't mean she's going to have a turn or anything. But ... perhaps we should try and quieten her down a little. It would be such a pity, if ...'

She wasn't able to finish, as Melissa returned just at that moment. But Tristan had got the message. And tragically it never entirely left him.

From that moment he found himself constantly watching and waiting for some slight abnormality in Melissa's behaviour ... a laugh when there was nothing to laugh at ... a solemn silence when he fancied her thoughts were wandering ... anything slightly out of key which did not entirely reflect his own attitude to art or life in general. Where before he'd taken no notice, he now observed minor things with gnawing suspicion, and looking back he saw how Martha had inveigled him into the forthcoming marriage.

Marriage!

And no children.

But how could he be expected to enter such an unfruitful commitment? He *wanted* children. Most men did: and if Melissa had been normal ... but she wasn't. The thought had never properly registered before. Now it did, and he was horrified, knowing that he couldn't possibly go through with things.

The trouble was, how to tell her. And her sister! ... how to break the news that after all, much as he loved Melissa, or *had*, and despite her own generosity, he did not feel justified, under the circumstances, of making her his wife.

He knew he couldn't, and after several sleepless nights decided the only course was a cooling off process. Broken dates through flimsy excuses, a lessening of passion when they met, withholding of kisses which had once meant so much to both of them, and an insistence that when they *did* go out together it would be a friendly foursome. Melissa was an intelligent girl; she couldn't fail to get the message if he played things that way.

She didn't

'What's the matter, dear?' Martha asked one late November afternoon as the yellow sky was deepening to evening, bringing a veil of rising mist to the suburbs.

'Nothing,' Melissa answered lifelessly. 'It's just that I wondered ... I thought Tristan was calling for me.' There was a pause before she added, 'He obviously isn't.'

She was standing staring out of the sitting room window overlooking the garden, so she didn't see the fleeting look of compressed triumph on her sister's plump countenance, or the brows arch almost gaily over the small eyes.

'Don't worry,' Martha said calmly. 'Men are often unpredictable. I must say your fiancé *has* appeared a trifle ... moody, shall we say, recently; neglectful's hardly the word to use; but one would have thought with so much ahead, your marriage, and finishing touches to the cottage to attend to, he'd have been just a *little* bit more attentive. Still ...' She shrugged her shoulders half contemptuously as Melissa turned, a bright glimmer of unshed tears in her eyes.

'Don't, Martha. *Don't*,' she said, rushing to the door. 'Do you mind not talking about Tristan ...'

'Of *course* not,' came the shocked reply just before the snap of the latch behind her sister's retreating form. 'And if I were you, Melissa, I'd stop fretting. No good will come of it, and you'll only get run down.'

Her words were prophetic.

At the beginning of December, Melissa developed an attack of flu which kept her in bed for a fortnight, leaving her at the end of it, wan and listless and very unlike the radiant girl Tristan had fallen in love with. During the illness he called once with a bunch of flowers, and sent a get-well card, simply signed

69

'Tristan'. But that was all. No suggestion of seeing her again or even wanting to. It was obvious to both Martha and Melissa that the affair was over.

'Well, if he's that type of man, the sooner you found out, the better,' Martha said over tea one day. 'I must confess I had my suspicions, the way he looked at *me* sometimes...' her voice trailed off suggestively.

'You?'

'Oh yes, dear,' Martha replied with underlying smugness. 'I *am* a woman, you know, and that fiancé of yours, or rather *ex* fiancé ... knew all the tricks I can assure you. Naturally I didn't say anything, but...'

'Stop, *stop*,' Melissa said, putting her hands to her ears. 'I can't bear it.'

'Oh *dear*,' contritely. 'Come now Melissa, it's clear you shouldn't be up yet. Flu *is* so lowering; and on top of that ... now come along. I'll help you upstairs, yes dear, yes. I insist.'

When Martha had that note in her voice Melissa knew there was no point in arguing; in any case she had no wish to, and allowed herself compliantly to be assisted to bed again, where she lay inert and miserable, unable fully to comprehend the terrible thing that had happened.

They had been so much in love. Their future had appeared so secure and without cloud.

How, she wondered, could he have deserted her the way he had without a word of explanation, just as though *her* feelings were so unimportant as to be completely ignored.

During the following week she suggested in a wild wave of hope that he might be ill. 'Couldn't you find out, *please*, Martha?' she begged.

'But there's no need, dear,' Martha replied coolly. 'He was seen yesterday by Mary, in the town, just outside the library.'

'Alone?'

Martha hesitated. Then she answered, 'Well, dear ... I'm afraid not. There was a girl with him.'

'A girl?'

'Oh dear. I *didn't want* to upset you. But now you know the truth I hope you'll pull yourself out of your dreary mood and try and get a little life into you. After all, you *still* have the cottage. You needn't live there, of course, I wouldn't agree to that, but what a marvellous place to paint in, Melissa ... it would be quite easy, as a matter of fact, to have the wall between the two bedrooms taken down, and convert the whole of the upstairs floor into a *studio*. Think of it! such a situation, with the woods behind and that stretch of common in front.'

'I should hate it,' Melissa said coldly. 'Sell it again Martha, unless you want it for yourself. It should fetch a good price.'

From then on, Melissa's health deteriorated rapidly, and shortly before Christmas the doctor confirmed that she had pleurisy of both lungs.

'Rest and extreme quiet will be necessary for a considerable time,' he told Martha. 'She should recover completely with the right treatment but this depression of hers doesn't help. By the way...'

'Yes?'

'She hasn't heard, I suppose, of the tragedy?'

'What tragedy?' Martha was genuinely bewildered.

'Do you mean you don't *know*? But my dear lady it was in the paper and on television last night...'

'I don't listen to the news,' Martha interrupted, 'except at ten occasionally. And I have no evening paper. Well, doctor, what's happened? Surely nothing that could concern my sister?'

'Oh dear, dear,' the doctor clicked his tongue against his teeth then resumed. 'Her fiancé...'

'*Ex*-fiancé if you don't mind.'

'Well, the young art teacher she was so fond of ... died yesterday. Very regrettable. There was a sit-in at the school, followed by one of these youthful riot affairs, and he was pushed ... or fell ... no one seems clear which at the moment ... over a balcony of the top corridor to the stone floor below. Death was instantaneous. It could hardly have been otherwise, with such an impact.'

Martha shuddered. 'How extremely shocking.'

'Yes.'

As he was leaving he turned at the door, saying, 'It would be better I think to keep the news from Melissa at the moment.'

A fleeting gleam like that of a cat's alighting on a dish of cream, flickered over Martha's face.

'Of *course*, doctor. I shan't say a word. There's no reason for her to know ... ever.'

'Oh but I hardly ...'

'Melissa will be very carefully looked after in future, doctor,' Martha told him. 'I don't intend her health and happiness to be risked a second time in decadent art circles. She and I will live quietly together here, or perhaps in the country, where no interference from the outside world can intrude ...' Her bosom was heaving; a curious glassy intensity lit her eyes. 'So you need have no fears that any word concerning that ... that unspeakable lay-about will ever come to her ears. Do you know he actually ... he actually tried something on *me* ...'

She paused breathlessly, then realising she might have gone too far, pulled herself together, and under a mask of self abnegation said, 'Oh, don't misunderstand me, he didn't *do* anything. But ... well, maybe I'm a bit

73

over-sensitive. Anything in the *slightest* lascivious, simply gives me the shudders. I expect...' half coyly, 'I'm just a little too old fashioned for the current everyday world.'

A moment later the doctor was striding down the path, knowing she was watching, and feeling discomforted by the whole interview.

The weather grew worse that night, and in the morning snow was falling, filming the trees and garden with thickening white. By evening all was cloaked into uniformity under a desolate lowering sky. Silence hugged everything into a brooding unease which even Martha found slightly unnerving.

Once or twice she went upstairs, hoping to have a little conversation with Melissa. But the girl lay inert and uninterested, her eyes turned to the window where snowflakes brushed the glass soundlessly, before breaking into ghostly powdered white.

'You should try and buck up,' Martha said, when she fetched Melissa's supper tray with the meal on it almost untouched. 'If you don't eat you'll never be any good. And what's the point of fretting about that ... that Tristan. He's *no good*, Melissa. For heaven's sake get that into your head once and for all. No good to any decent girl.'

With which parting shot she went out, snapping the door sharply to, behind her.

After taking the tray to the kitchen she returned to the small sitting room at the front of the house, and switched on the television, all three channels in turn. But there was nothing she liked ... only a woman droning on about obscenity laws on one, with a lurid Western as alternative, and on the other a gyrating female screaming her head off.

Martha switched off abruptly, went to the window and drew the curtains aside. It was still snowing, and difficult now to distinguish the path leading from the gate to the front door. The road beyond was quite obscured, the bushes emerging only as slightly shadowed humps under the trees. Nothing moved. Not even a bird ... until ... suddenly, with a queer unreasoning feeling of apprehension pricking her skull, Martha saw it ... a figure moving steadily forward towards the house, bare head thrust forward, chin huddled against the elements into the furred collar of a snow flecked wind-cheater. There was something purposeful about him ... a sense of deadly mission that chilled her to the bone. She wouldn't see him. *No.* It wasn't natural for *anyone* to call at such an hour in such weather, except for the doctor. And Martha knew it wasn't him. The form was too tall, too young. If Tristan had been alive ... but Tristan had died yesterday. So it couldn't possibly be Tristan.

She closed the curtains quickly and hurried into the hall to see the catch of the front door was safely down. You could never tell these days what queer characters were lurking round. There were so many lay-abouts, hippies, drug fiends and murderers on the loose, it was one's duty always to be alert and on the safe side.

Her hand was already near the lock, when the door, of its own accord seemingly, swung open slowly, before she had time to snap it to.

She stepped back, one hand to her mouth, noting the cold stare of blue eyes more glassy than iced pools, and far far more condemning. His fair beard was frozen and stiff; he walked soundlessly, following her retreating figure down the hall with a stiff purposeful gait as though dragged from death itself.

And then she knew.

'Don't,' she muttered, with chattering teeth, and a queer cotton-wool feeling about her legs. 'Tristan. Tristan ... don't ... don't ...'

He didn't speak at first. Just bared his lips in the semblance of a grin already holding the macabre quality of a skeleton's grimace. Then in a harsh whisper that could have been the wind's soughing round the old house, but clear, damningly clear in Martha's ears, he said, 'I've come for Melissa. Where is Melissa?'

She swallowed hard, trying to control the violent pumping of her heart, clutching at a chair for support, her terrified mind searching wildly for escape, for help from someone ... anyone, Mary, the au pair, but no sound came from her lips, and her limbs wouldn't move.

Like an automaton, she watched him go to the foot of the stairs and lift his head, felt a rush of icy wind on her face when he called in that sibilant icy voice ... 'Melissa ... I'm here. Come down, my darling...'

There was the thin sound of a door creaking above; a flutter of movement, and an elongated reflected shadow from landing to stairs, before Melissa, in a white nightdress with her luxurious hair loose about her shoulders appeared at the top. She paused briefly, her luminous eyes wide and intent upon Tristan ... or that which seemed to be Tristan. Then, slowly and proudly, very erect, with her arms stretched before her in the manner of a sleepwalker, she moved quietly down each tread until, at the foot, she drew level with he who had come to claim her.

Martha gave a queer muffled scream, huddling herself against the wall as they passed, trying desperately to call her sister's name, but unable to formulate the word.

Quietly they drifted through the doorway into the cold snow outside, and as quietly merged into the whiteness of earth and sky, of freezing air and enveloping curtain of the waiting night. Then the door closed, as it had opened, of its own volition, leaving Martha alone in the dark hall.

For a time, how long she didn't know, she remained slumped there, shuddering not only from fright and the sudden nerveless chill of her body, but from the memory of those eyes ... the clear cold merciless eyes so full of hatred and ruthless condemnation.

At last, when movement returned to her limbs, she got to her feet and clutching at the bannister dragged herself upstairs and along the landing to her sister's room.

She waited a moment outside, and then went in.

Melissa was lying in the bed, one hand near her throat just above the breast. The other had fallen limply over the side, slender fingers greenish-white in the eerie bluish glow from the window. Hunched up like a frightened animal, Martha approached and tentatively touched it.

Then she screamed.

Screamed and screamed so the sound echoed through every room and corridor of the house, high pitched and shrill, until at last it died into the low drawn-out howl of an animal in mortal pain.

When found by the servants, she was lying grotesquely twisted up on the floor, one hand caught in the counterpane of her sister's bed. Even in death her eyes were rigid and staring, holding such jealousy and possessive hatred, the au pair, with a shudder, found a cloth to cover it.

The doctor was called and arrived half an hour later.

'A stroke, poor thing,' he said after a brief examination of the body, 'which the autopsy will prove, I'm sure. As for this poor girl . . .' he shook his head regretfully following the usual medical routine, 'no one can do anything for her now. She must have died . . . as far as I can judge, some time before her sister. Such a pity. A lovely girl.'

He did not add what would have been the truth, but hardly etiquette, that Melissa should never have been left to the care of her half-sister, the crazy Miss Marriott. Neither did he say that Martha had died in a fit, just as her mother had before her. There'd been a taint in the first Mrs Marriott's family, which he well knew. But such an unpleasant detail of family history had really no bearing on either death . . . so far as he was aware . . .

There was much of course he *didn't* know, and with Melissa and Tristan gone the true facts would never be revealed, which perhaps was as well, according to the old adage 'let the dead bury the dead'.

A popular saying often trivially thrown out to dispel an unpleasant subject.

But do the dead really die? Or is it that sometimes they can return under propitious circumstances to haunt the terrain of their earthly existences? Whatever the answer the fact remains that since that tragic snowbound night, Four Towers has been untenanted. A few have stayed there for a day or two, but never more than a week, the reason for such sudden departures being generally described as 'faulty acoustics', 'queer draughts', and 'a whispering sound along the landings', with something white 'flitting down the stairs'.

Others, passing by the gates on a winter's evening have imagined the front door to open quietly, and shadowed figures drift through.

Imagination?

But what *is* that?

No one yet has been able to give a full and completely satisfactory meaning of the word. And it is doubtful if anyone ever will. Some things are beyond explanation; in which category Four Towers now belongs.

CHAPTER FIVE

FALSIES

I would never have expected it of Oliver; never for one moment, or of course being the type of woman I am, with finesse and a certain delicacy about certain matters, I'd not have married him.

It just shows doesn't it, that you never can tell.

I suppose at my time of life ... not getting on exactly, or elderly ... but middle-aged, in the prime of life as they put it, I was taken momentarily off balance, and jumped into wedlock not wisely but too well. Or perhaps too thoughtlessly puts it better.

Let me explain at the very beginning of this rather macabre and disturbing story, that I've always been a great reader. So living on my own in my nice suburban semi-detached house that had been left to me by my mother, I was a frequent visitor to our district library, where I spent hours every week delving into books, historical mostly, or autobiographies of famous people which took me whirling away from prosaic everyday life into realms of unbelievable experience and romance.

It was wonderful, and so stimulating, after the wearying business of buying a chop at the butchers, or queuing at a stores simply to purchase a few odds and ends of cheese and packet soup and a loaf of bread in a *really* fresh condition—you know the sort of thing—to relax into the warmth and confines of a more cultural sphere. And the girls there were generally so helpful except for one toffee-nosed young woman with a bun on top of her head and a curvacious out-in-front, out-behind figure that showed only too obviously she wasn't interested in literature at *all*. No *dedication*. No seeking for knowledge or wishing to impart it. Just *one* thing ... S.E.X. Oh yes, I knew her type. And she knew I knew it. Her stare as I handed her my book and ticket expressed just one emotion ... contempt.

I wanted to tell her where she got off, the silly thing, but I didn't, naturally. Dignity came first; so I generally managed an acid smile, with a 'thank you', slight incline of the head, and then went out.

Well, all this is really beside the point, except that it was there, in the sanctum of the library that I met Oliver. Oliver William Wigsley, to be correct. He was down in Seacarne for a prolonged holiday, following his retirement from some bank or other up country.

It would not be correct to say we 'clicked' immediately. We didn't. In the first place he was an extremely short rather tubby man, whereas I'm tall and thin, with features to match, and being rather short-sighted was apt to miss everything about him except the top of his balding head when I passed by. One day, however, I stumbled over his foot— incidentally he had *very* large feet—and as he helped me up we were face to face for the first time.

Is it true I wonder that opposites are naturally drawn to each other? Or is it really the reverse, a sort of challenge to prove oneself?

I don't know. Even now I'm amazed how quickly we became acquainted following that first brief meeting. I found him charming; quite *charming* ... and such a knowledgeable man, with an interest in a host of subjects I'd never even taken a peep into. That's what intrigued me ... in the beginning. That and the fact that he obviously appreciated my studious nature, and commended my taste for delving into the lives of the famous, and historical romances of the crowned heads of Europe ... especially the scandalous early Georges of the last century, with their bevies of mistresses and illicit loves.

Oh, I'm not narrow minded; indeed I think one should *know* about such things, however virtuous one's personal life is. And I was certainly *that*. Virtuous I mean; I'd been brought up to it, and anyway my outward appearance was not the vulgar tempting kind; nor ever could have been with my proportions. All my life I'd told myself it didn't matter, it was *character* that counted. And I believe this still to be true. But I must admit that as my new friendship with Oliver William Wigsley deepened I succumbed to a few titivating little vanities and indulgences that I'd never dreamed of doing before. For instance I bought a new skirt and a most elegant blouse which I found looked far smarter with a pair of discreet 'falsies' underneath.

Falsies! can you imagine it! *Me*. It was quite an ordeal going into the underwear department of our one store and *asking*. But when I left, with the pink and blue striped paper bag under my arm I felt really exhilarated for a few minutes, a 'bit of a devil' as they say in those racy magazine stories; and this lured me on to other things. I had my hair permed.

My knees were shaking when I left the salon. But I knew the bunchiness suited me better than the bun, and the assistant had assured me that in a little time the fuzz would develop into gentle softening waves.

So that's how it all started. You could write up my whole biography of those eventful six months I suppose in three words ... 'books! falsies! marriage'.

Yes. I married Oliver William Wigsley in June following our first meeting in Seacarne public library the previous January, and together we took up our connubial life in my late mother's house.

Perhaps that was a mistake. I don't know. It

might have been wiser on my part to have allowed him ... or *insisted* he used some of the shares he was always referring to, for a new dwelling; ... a bungalow, or pleasant semi-detached in another district to give us a clean start. If I'd done that I mightn't be sitting at a window of this dreary place now with only a few sparrows to watch striking at the glass, and that odious monkey-tree poking from the scrubby lawn. In fact I'm sure I wouldn't, because Oliver wouldn't have married me. He was a 'close' one, you see, with a lot of worldly ambitions beneath that rotund holier-than-thou exterior, whereas I, mature in years, was a complete softy in the ways of the world.

Oh, he was clever; but the way he manipulated it, getting me to 'Brighthouse' of all places, still gives me the shivers when I think of it.

Not that they're *unkind* to me here exactly, although at times I must admit I want to lunge out—and what an *unladylike* term—*lunge*; not a bit like me; ... but it's their *condescension* you see ...! '*Now* Miss Wigsley dear, how are we today? Going to be a good girl, are we?'

We! did you ever hear such nonsense; as though there were *three* or four of me?

Sometimes I draw myself up to my full five feet nine inches, and say in my Duchess voice, 'Kindly remove your person and leave me to my own devices. I wish to think.' It's a speech I've concocted through the months to quell their impertinence. But does it work? Oh, no, indeed. Simply because they're so ignorant. Why, do you know ... there's not a book in the place I'd deign to look at, not with a barge-pole; although come to think of it a barge-pole could be a handy weapon occasionally ... if only for smashing their awful window, enabling me to crawl down a drain pipe or something. The trouble is, of course, the bars.

Bars! sometimes the awful horror of it, the *indignity*, sweeps over me, and I could weep. Not only because of myself, but *Oliver*—that he could have resorted to such evil practice.

There! it's out. *Evil*. Yes, I'm afraid it's true; in the end Oliver William Wigsley proved himself to be no more than a devil's disciple. And didn't Bernard Shaw or someone refer to just such a term? In a play I think. But I can't quite place it now, and certainly *he* could never have been *anyone* like Oliver.

When I look back, the 'falsies' seemed to be at the root of our marital trouble and my great disillusionment; although of course incompatibility must have been there at the very beginning. I mean, although we had a very nice wedding, at a Registry Office—*not* a church, Oliver had a 'thing' against religion and 'show' as he called it—with a small reception in the Bull and Trumpet, afterwards—*his* choice, I detest public houses—our wedding night was certainly not the inspiring experience I'd *imagined*.

I'd expected him at least to kiss me with the gentle passion any 'nice' woman expects of her bridegroom, and to say just *once* even 'I love you', instead of going over the whole sordid business of stocks and shares and wills and things that really *do* take the edge off romantic yearnings and aspirations.

But he didn't.

Oh no, not once. All I got was a crude nip of the bottom, when he'd finished his business thesis—and it really *was* a thesis, I can tell you—and a sudden nasty tweak of my falsies, which pinged, like a pricked balloon, and fell off.

I'd *never* felt so embarrassed in my life. You see I'd planned everything so carefully. When we'd undressed I thought, very modestly in the dark, I'd pull my almost see-through (but not quite) nightdress over my head, and slip into bed quietly, removing them before he noticed.

That's what I'd *thought*. But with Oliver being so rough and I'm afraid more than a little 'over the eight', I hadn't a chance, and was left simply standing there, in my suspender belt and panties; ... actually they were rather pretty, pink with frills, ... and *no bosoms* at all. Just flat chicken-breasted me, with Oliver William Wigsley staring as though he was at a peep show, or zoo or something.

My hair was all right of course; and in that awful moment I made the best of it, shaking my head, and lifting my chin as much like those

87

television and magazine advertisements as I could, hoping to distract him from those two pear-shaped objects lying at my feet.

But it was no use. He looked first at me then at them, and started to *laugh*.

His laughter unnerved me; it was so contemptuous and *prolonged*. And hurtful too.

But Oliver didn't care about that. And it's my conviction now that when he found he couldn't get his fist on my bit of capital, he just went on hurting me as much as he could, so that eventually he'd drive me off my head.

He made them think he had, too, in the end. At least not *him*, it was just me. Oh he had a persuasive tongue, Oliver William Wigsley; and what with that and the dabbling—but I haven't said anything about the dabbling yet, have I? A great omission on my part, because of course *without* it he'd have got nowhere.

Yes. Oliver *dabbled*—or *concentrated* if you like—on all those unhealthy things like hypnotism, Yoga, black magic, auto-suggestion, the whole lot. And don't say there's nothing wrong in it. There *is*.

My position, and where I am now, proves it.

He was also, and still is, I've no doubt, a man of decidedly lascivious nature, or he'd never have resorted to materialising what he did ... those *breasts*!

Oh I realise how ridiculous it must seem, put on paper, but those falsies started to *haunt* me. Not as *falsies* you understand? ... But the

88

real thing.

B.R.E.A.S.T.S.

Just one at first, an obscene looking luminous shape, like a fat pear with an electric light bulb inside it glowing above my bed. I'd gone upstairs early one night because I had a headache, switched my lamp off and closed my eyes tight to get peace and quiet, and would you believe it, when I opened them for a moment, there it was—a juicy shining object that hovered and almost smirked—if a breast can be said to smirk; then it slowly descended to the tip of my nose, hanging lusciously there for a moment or two, with its pointed pink nipple tickling and squeaking ... yes, I'm sure it squeaked before rising again disintegrating into nothing.

Oh dear, oh dear. I felt positively faint, and put my head under the bedclothes until Oliver came up, after a spell no doubt, of his wicked meditation.

I didn't say anything though, not then. But later, when it happened again, not once but twice, and after that at any odd moment when I was off guard, I naturally *had* to.

'*Stop* it, Oliver,' I told him firmly, but in what I hoped was a perfectly controlled manner. '*Stop* it, do you hear?'

Oliver looked astonished. It was a way he had of discomforting me when he was in the wrong, making him look falsely innocent like a round-eyed elderly boy with his button mouth slightly open, and his pale blue eyes staring.

'*Me?*' He said, 'What do you mean, Flossie? I didn't do anything, not anything at *all.*'

'You know what I mean very well,' I answered sharply, 'and don't call me Flossie. *Florence* is my name. The name I was christened by ... Florence Victoria, if you must know.' And I drew my head up with befitting dignity.

But there was nothing dignified in Oliver's reaction; oh *no.* His professed cultural sense ... as I'd already discovered ... was merely a 'front' and a lie.

'I *see,*' he said, with quite a nasty undertone in his voice. 'Very well, madam. Florence *Victoria!*' and then he laughed. 'Oh my holy aunt. Whatever next, I ask you? So what is it I'm commanded to stop, your majesty?' And he bowed his head slightly, 'If I may humbly enquire?'

Now sticking to my guns, with Oliver William Wigsley in such a mood, was no easy matter. But I did it.

'Stop your disgusting habit of resurrecting things,' I told him, 'Especially *that.*'

'What?'

It was really most distasteful having to answer, 'You know very well ... that ... that *obscenity*! that *breast.*'

There. It was out. I took a deep breath, and turned away so Oliver wouldn't see the red staining my face. A flush can be becoming

90

when you're young. But at *my* age, well, you know how people are, always on the watch for *one* thing, that obnoxious word 'the change', which can not only be discomforting to one's equilibrium, but *dangerous* ... especially with anyone like Oliver William Wigsley who I knew by then was plotting to get me unhinged. 'My poor wife,' I could imagine him saying with one finger to his temple, shaking his head significantly, 'Sad, so very sad. Her age you know.'

Age? My foot. *He* knew what he was up to all right, and so did I.

'Did you hear me?' I went on when he didn't answer, '*Breast*?'

'Yes, my dear,' he replied, then very meekly ... far *too* meekly. 'I heard.'

'Well then?'

'You must be mad, Flossie ... I mean Florence,' he said as calmly as you could get. 'I'm not that clever I'm afraid; if I was you'd have more than one of them floating about the ether.'

Oh the impudence of it. I was quite aghast. But do you know ... that's *just what happened*.

The next day was a little foggy, and when Oliver had gone for his morning pint to the Legion, I got the fright of my life. It was a 'stew day' ... I generally make a stew from the left-overs from the joint the day before ... and as I took the dish out of the oven to give the vegetables a bit of a poke and prod, you know how it is, to see everything was cooking properly ... there they were, floating above the grill ... like a couple of most unheavenly twins ... *two* of them, pink and plump, and squeaking with glee, their nipples positively *rosy*. I put the casserole dish down with a shudder, held my hands to my ears, closed my eyes for a moment, and fled from the kitchen into the lounge, wondering if I was in for a stroke or something, or if ... just *if*, ... I had imagined it, as there was steam about, and there *had* been a bit of a 'fug' in the air, what with the cooking and the mist outside.

But it wasn't that.

When I looked up again I saw with a shock and fluttering of my heart, they'd followed me, and were hovering suspended over the sideboard, smug, and bulbous, although a bit furry looking, but obviously what they were ... B.R.E.A.S.T.S. The *ghosts* of breasts if you like, but then that made it somehow worse, because ghosts can appear at any odd time can't they? And in any old way, through doors, walls, windows, and at most disconcerting moments, calculated to give the maximum shock.

And of course that's exactly what occurred.

Following the first time I was *always* seeing them; well, perhaps not *always*. There were days at a time when they didn't appear at all, and I'd think perhaps it was over, and Oliver had stopped his dabbling. Unfortunately he hadn't; and when everything seemed most normal, I'd know from his expression he was *concentrating*. He'd be very quiet, and sort of watchful ... watchful in a particularly ominous kind of way as though waiting for something.

I guessed what it was, naturally. Those breasts. The phantom vulgar things he'd created from his own sick mind, just because I, through no fault of my own, hadn't been born with any ... well, not any to speak of.

'Vegetables, Oliver?' I'd say in businesslike tones, handing him the brussels sprouts. 'Come along now; greens are good for you. Help the liver; and don't tell me you're not liverish ... you wouldn't moon about so much if you weren't.'

Oh yes, in spite of his secret abhorrent practices, I really *did* do my best to help him.

But it was no good.

Oliver William Wigsley and the Breasts United were too strong eventually for me to combat. And the climax was really quite awful, but the one no doubt that my unprincipled spouse had been counting on from the very beginning of our marriage when my falsies fell off ... or even perhaps before that. It's impossible to say with men of his calibre.

Anyway, as Oliver's birthday approached I planned to throw down the gauntlet, and make one last effort at reconciliation, so he'd end his malicious etheric experiments, and perhaps allow us to settle down in a normal way. Normal for *us* probably describes it better.

93

For three days I hadn't seen the breasts ... the last time had been in an evening, poking round the bathroom door, when I was having a nice soak, all smothered in foamy sweet smelling bubbles that are supposed to make a woman desirable. You know the sort of thing.

Well, I was not only scared, but really *annoyed*. Because after all, my bathtime had become by then the only peaceful indulgence in my life. So I jumped up, nearly slipped, and threw the sponge at the two beastly prying things. They burst like two fat bubbles just as the door opened, and Oliver's face appeared, taking the impact of the sponge flat on his face.

'My dear!' he gasped, in the hypocritical way I hated. 'What's wrong? Are you all right?'

'What do I *look* like?' I gasped. 'What do *you* think?'

He didn't reply. Perhaps it was as well he didn't, because of course I shouldn't have asked such a leading question. So I went on quickly, 'You can't leave them alone, can you? Or me?'

'What, my dear?'

'Those ... those unspeakable things, the breasts,' I shouted, quite loudly.

Oliver didn't say anything, just disappeared, shutting the door behind him.

I thought for the rest of the week my temper and contempt combined with the sponge—after all my aim had appeared very smart, even though it hadn't been for him exactly—*might* have worked the trick. He really did appear a little more understanding following the unpleasant little scene which is why I went to the trouble of arranging the birthday party.

'You shall have a proper celebration,' I told him, 'cake and everything...' forgetting temporarily he was a man instead of just a tubby grown-up looking kind of boy. 'Wouldn't that be nice, Oliver? And ask *any*one ... any friends you like. I shall invite Selina Prague of course, as she's such an old friend, but that's all. The day is to be yours, Oliver, and yours alone.'

Which was almost true.

But not *quite*.

Because you see, just when I had the knife ready to cut Oliver's birthday cake, following a hearty rendering of that old song 'Twenty one today', by two of his pals, a publican and a rather bawdy journalist ... not *my* choice of company at all ... but typical of male club life I'm afraid ... *they* appeared.

Quite suddenly.

The two of them.

Pink, plump, powdered and painted for the occasion, with little daisies round the nipples, and frills of lace puffing them up *abnormally*. Oh! it was *disgusting*. And with Selina there too. Selina, who was so prim and refined, and had probably never *seen* such a thing before. There they were, squeaking and dancing, sort of floating up and down above the cake, and me with my knife poised ... well! I ask you. Can you blame me for what happened? Naturally I thrust the weapon at the cheeky things; and when they escaped, rising together towards the ceiling, I jumped on the table, striking this way and that, calling Oliver wildly to help me.

But no one did.

Not even the vulgar publican who was broad and strong and should have been smart enough from all his dart-throwing, to catch such obviously bulbous creatures.

Just no one.

That's what so often happens though isn't it, when a crisis is concerned? No one wants to be involved.

And no one was ... except Oliver.

Such a tale he made of it to the doctor and authorities who obviously all considered him a most unfortunate man, and were therefore willing to help in any way they could.

The help he got was to have me certified, enabling him also to have control of my shares, doling out what is necessary of my income from time to time to keep me in this place.

Why Selina didn't stick up for me I really don't know. But then Selina fainted at the most dramatic moment, and all she said when they questioned her was ... 'The knife. The knife ... she could've *murdered* us all.'

Murder? As if I would. I'm the gentlest of women under normal conditions, bearing no

96

grudge to anyone really, not even Oliver William Wigsley who was in reality rather a pitiful creature with his fancies and lustful thoughts.

No. I don't blame Oliver any more. Just *them* . . . the *breasts*. And if either of them come within a yard of me . . . well, it's then I see red, and then only.

I'll get them one day, you see.

The trouble is not being allowed a knife and fork, my actions are so very limited.

If only they'd let me have a mirror, I could keep watch for the first sign of them materialising behind my shoulder. But they won't. No glass. Nothing but plastic.

The only pleasure I have, actually, is watching the sparrows peck at the window, and I wish then I could open it just a teeny bit to give them a few crumbs.

The darlings.

CHAPTER SIX

NEVER AT SUNSET

'Not down theer,' the old man said shaking his head solemnly. 'Doan' 'ee go theer, surr ... never at sunset.'

With this sombre warning he passed me, turned, and took the corner to the left leading down into Bradmarsh where I was staying for a few days before continuing my walking tour of the West Country.

I looked down the hill to the village at the bottom. It appeared pleasant and harmless enough; in fact quite intriguing with its huddle of cottages and church spire tipped with the rosy gold of fading sunlight.

Though enclosed by the violent shadows of the humped hills on either side, the view was clear enough to give a snaking glimmer of river under an arched bridge where a large house stood, half submerged by trees. I could also define further on a threadwork of narrow streets running haphazardly from a central square.

There seemed no movement anywhere; but then in the fitful light I'd not see it if there was.

A perfectly normal country hamlet surely? Old and in character with its remote surroundings, and just the type of place I was interested in. A bit late in the day perhaps for a proper survey, but time enough for a quick glance round before the stipulated dinner hour at the pub-cum-hotel where I was staying.

So I started down, walking sharply, and shrugging off the old man's dour warning as a mere local superstition, or perhaps even a corny joke thought up to titivate interest, and a sense of his own importance.

He'd looked a bit of a character in his too-long coat, corded trousers tied at the ankles, and weathered felt hat pushed over his grey locks almost to the ears. A retired farm labourer possibly, or even some eccentric intellectual living the life of a hermit tucked away from the company of his own kind.

His background was not important anyway, and when I neared the valley all thought of him and his dire forebodings were completely swept from my mind. The vista, still lit by the lingering glow of a fading sky, held an enchantment and enchanting quality that led me to pause briefly before going ahead into the village itself.

On my right, just before the bridge, the house I'd noticed from above at the cross roads, stood mellowed and gracious looking behind a stretch of lawn sloping to the river's edge. A few trees fringed the garden, thickening at the back of the building into darkening woodland which was already sending long fingered shadows across the grass.

100

Everything was very still and silent, until a wild cry, followed by a girl's soft laughter—or so it seemed—shattered the uncanny quiet.

I went a step nearer and saw a peacock strutting over the lawn, wonderful tail outspread fan-wise, as though to secrete all the colours of that perfect dying day. A white-clad figure followed; that of a young girl, obviously, in a flimsy frock, the tip of her fair head touched to momentary molten gold from the sun's last rays. Then I heard a woman's voice, gentle, and very sweet, almost *too* sweet, calling, 'Iris ... Iris ...'

The girl turned, and went slowly, gracefully towards the door of the house, with the bird following.

A queer sense of unreality fell on me, with a compelling desire to know more about those who lived there. Although I'd not seen her face clearly, I knew intuitively the girl was beautiful, and during the brief interim of unavowed communication, could sense she was half aware of my presence. Once she glanced over her shoulder in my direction giving a momentary glimpse of pale profile; then her form was taken into the light and shade of early evening, leaving me curiously reluctant to go without meeting her face to face.

I searched wildly through my mind for an acceptable excuse to warrant intrusion, and decided it wasn't necessary. Any faked up explanation would somehow be an affront to the magic of the place and the day's dying beauty. The gate leading directly from the road, skirting the lawn to the house, was already half ajar, as though inviting entry; and a path wound along the river bank that would obviously be used by anyone wanting solitude, or an afternoon's fishing perhaps.

So without further hesitation I plunged through, ducking my head to avoid a few interlaced branches of sapling trees, and was almost immediately on the verge of the lawn.

The peacock was strutting towards another at the opposite side of the garden, and an elderly woman in a black dress and apron, was carrying a tray of tea-things from a summerhouse nearby. She turned simultaneously with the girl, as I approached, then went into the house shaking her head disapprovingly. A moment later a tall figure appeared in the doorway, paused for a second or two, then came to meet me. She was slim, erect, and wearing grey, a shade darker than her hair. I couldn't judge her age, but quite clearly she was the girl's mother. The likeness, even from a distance, was unmistakable, although the elder, in contrast to her daughter's apparent shyness, had an imperious grace that at first took me aback.

'I'm sorry,' I said hesitantly when she drew near. 'I didn't mean to intrude. I . . .'

The perfectly formed mouth which had been so set a moment before, relaxed into a smile, quite disarming me.

'It doesn't matter,' she said, with serene sweetness. 'You have nothing to apologise for. We do get strangers from time to time. And it's nice for Iris to see someone young for a change instead of just her elderly doting mother and the servants.'

The way she said 'elderly doting mother' somehow asked for a compliment, and I gave it.

'You don't seem elderly at all,' I told her gallantly, which was quite true. 'In fact ...' the words trailed off uncertainly. I felt suddenly very young, naive, and stupid.

She patted my hand gently, and I noticed with surprise that she wore gloves, very pale grey tightly fitting gloves, probably suede. I don't know why that fact should have registered so clearly, except its suggestiveness of another period and age in time. But it did; and as the moments ticked by the meeting, more than ever, assumed a sense of unreality, of belonging to a dream-state rather than one of flesh and blood. Yet the pressure of her hand was solid enough, the grass under my feet held the fresh sweet tang of spring. The distant echoes of voices from the back of the house intermingled with the cooing of doves and intermittent screaming of the peacocks, were all real sounds making tangible impact on the air, more vividly recorded because of the extreme silence around.

Yes. The aura of quietness where normally surely so many small sighs, scufflings, and creakings of nature should have been was strange, even a little awesome. Not even a stirring from the river nearby. No plop of water vole, no gentle flutter of a bird's wing from the trees. Only, when I strained my ears, the faintest lapping of water as though from another dimension of existence, the thin distant crying of the peacocks of course, and the murmur of the woman in grey saying, 'Iris dear, don't be frightened. What's the matter with you, child? Come here and meet our visitor, Mr . . .?'

'Carne,' I replied quickly, 'Richard Carne.' Adding stupidly, 'I'm at university. I take my degree in the autumn.'

The smile deepened, as the girl moved tentatively with the grace of a young fawn towards us.

'Richard then,' the soft cultured voice continued. 'Richard and Iris.'

I held out my hand, enclosing the girl's for a fraction of time, feeling the delicate structure of bones, the cool flower-like impact of delicate skin pulsing beneath my grip.

Then I released it suddenly, as a quick streak of last sunlight flooded her face to rose. The elder woman's mood seemed to change abruptly. Her spine stiffened. Gentleness faded into an air of severity as she continued in remote cold tones, 'I'm sorry you did not come a little earlier. This is the time we retire.'

Her dismissal of me was so painfully obvious I couldn't help remarking with more spirit than I felt, 'I didn't want to intrude. I apologise. I should have known I was trespassing.'

'But you weren't, you weren't! Please come again . . .'

The plea was so soft, so anguished, I wondered at first if I'd imagined it. But one glance at the girl's face affirmed I hadn't.

The lips were parted slightly, eyes brilliantly dark in the quickly fading light, so intense upon me I had an impulse to defy her mother and pause there until the quiet dusk had enfolded and drained the last daylight away. I even ventured a step forward. But the tall austere figure seemed to expand and dominate all natural terrain. Her bearing and manner were so compulsive, the younger frail image of the girl was swamped for a few moments and obliterated from the scene.

How long the confrontation lasted between us, I've now no idea. It could have been seconds or minutes. But when at last I managed to drag my eyes from the condemning stare, Iris was gone, leaving behind only the darkening garden through which a shivering breeze was already moaning in the undergrowth, and the elongated figure of the woman receding towards the dim silhouette of the house.

I turned quickly and hurried back down the path to the gate. When I looked back no streak of crimson or fading gold lit the sky. All was chill and grey, deepening to uncertain uniformity as a film of mist billowed insidiously over the grass, hovering shroud-like upon paths and undergrowth in curdling contorted shapes.

Pausing for a few moments I saw, from the house, a square of window lit suddenly by a wan glare of bluish light that zig-zagged tremblingly over the lawn, catching my eyes as though a torch had been switched there. A second later it had gone, but as I crossed to the road it was with a strange sensation of being watched; and I was aware for the first time how quickly early twilight was fading into night.

Besides being intrigued I was uneasy, perhaps even a little afraid, though there was no apparent reason for it. A beautiful girl living in a benighted great house with an over-possessive mother—not a unique situation surely? But in this case there had seemed something slightly off-beat ... out of key.

Everything, the wild crying of the peacocks, and unexpected appearance of the ethereal looking Iris, followed by the mother's inexplicable change of mood after her first pleasant welcome, held the quality more of some unexplainable fairy tale than down-to-earth reality. And 'down-to-earth' was an incongruous term to use under the circumstances.

I walked up the road to the turn where the lane cut down abruptly again towards Bradmarsh, and the pub where I was staying. There was no sign of the old man. Except for a few sheep in a field the whole countryside appeared deserted, and from the dark sky above the furred mist, I knew I'd taken far longer than I'd thought over the brief interview. The glimmer of lights in the valley was welcoming. Already I was chilled by the damp and night air, and looking forward to a meal, knowing though, that my late arrival would bring disapproving glances from 'mine host' and his wife. Like most country places, I guessed a break in routine might mean staff problems.

And I was right.

'I'm afraid there's nothing hot now.' The woman said with a glance at the clock. 'Eight-thirty. And the day girl's already gone. Still there's cold meat, and I can perhaps put on more soup...'

'Oh don't worry, please,' I answered. 'I don't want to inconvenience you. I should have paid more attention to time. But I was caught up in conversation,' I paused before adding, 'at the large house by the river.'

'What large house?' The tones were abrupt, the broad countenance suddenly alert and interested. Shrewd, yet somehow fearful.

'In the valley. Down the hill to the left, going from this way.'

'Oh.' Whether that one word was meant to shut me up, I wasn't certain. But I knew beyond doubt I'd caught her unawares, broached a topic she'd no wish to pursue, so I persisted by enquiring, 'Who lives there? Do you know?'

'Of course. Torrence is the name. A Mrs Torrence. Rather a peculiar woman. Shuts herself away you could say. We don't bother with such people round here.'

She would have passed me by quickly if I hadn't touched her arm. 'No. Please, I won't keep you a moment. It was the daughter who impressed me. She seemed so . . .'

'*Daughter?* There's no daughter.' The flat statement delivered in such blunt, almost deadly tones, took me aback.

'I'm sorry. *What* did you say? About there being no daughter?'

'There isn't. And if you spoke to anyone . . . anyone else except Mrs Torrence, it was a servant or something.'

'The girl was called Iris,' I persisted, 'and she was certainly no *servant*.'

'Well then, I'm afraid I can't help you. And if you'll excuse me now I *have* got things to attend to.'

Snubbed, and realising I had appeared to be making an issue of a rather unimportant point—from *her* point of view anyway—I said

108

formally, 'Of course. I'm sorry to have delayed you.'

But the feeling of curiosity and lingering bewilderment remained in my mind. My landlady's reluctance and ambiguity concerning a perfectly normal line of questioning haunted me during the hours that followed. And when morning came I decided to stay on at Bradmarsh for the next few days, making another call at the house when the hour and weather were propitious. Unfortunately an early mist soon turned to thin grey rain later, which did not lift until the afternoon. Wearing a windcheater because the air was cold with a flurry of driving wind, I set off about three thirty with some trumped up excuse ready, in case I was unwelcomed, that I'd lost my pocket book, not an important possession, but one I treasured for sentimental reasons.

White lies were not generally my line of approach but in this case I'd no conscience. A little poking about in the trees and along the path could harm no one. And if the elegant Mrs Torrence thought I was trespassing she would soon send me packing with an aristocratic 'flea-in-my-ear'.

I had an idea she'd be watching from one of the windows.

What gave me the impression I don't know ... probably the recollection of silence, of extreme windless quiet and suspension of time which had intensified the atmosphere of that first strange meeting. Whatever the cause I knew I had to face it, somehow make further contact with the lovely Iris whose fawn-like elusive grace had so enchanted me.

Perhaps at this point I should clarify certain points about myself at that period. As I've said, I was young, but was considered well balanced, and not unduly romantic, though I'd known a fair number of girls and women, and already experienced two love-affairs which had ended abruptly with a certain amount of disillusionment. This though was different. As I didn't know the girl I could hardly be in love, but I was too near the danger-point not to realise how easy this would be, and that I wanted it at that moment more than anything else in the world, so I found myself automatically hurrying as I reached the base of the hill, half running when the river came into view.

By then the fine rain had abated a little. But the slender trees looked wan and sad against the grey background. It seemed incredible almost that only the day before peacocks had walked proudly over the velvet lawn in the fading sunlight, beside a girl in a shimmering white dress, tumbled bright hair about her shoulders catching all the colours of the rainbow.

'Iris,' I thought with sudden longing... 'Iris, Iris...' recalling Milton's words in *Comus*...

110

Iris there, with humid bow,
Waters the odorous banks that blow
Flowers of more mingled hew
Than her purpl'd scarf can shew

And I'd thought myself no romantic. Yet there I was conjuring up the lines of a long dead poet as though sensing beauty for the first time.
Ridiculous really.
Or ... was it?
As I pushed through the frail spinney of saplings the cold light seemed to lift a little, and when I reached the stretch of lawn a beam of silver penetrated the greyness, falling slantwise across the face of the house.
I stopped involuntarily, under a strange compulsion, my eyes riveted on the Georgian frontage, half fearing, yet *knowing*, that someone or *something* would presently materialise through the blurred light.
And then I saw it ... a pale set visage emerging gradually from the shadowed interior to a square of window on the right of the door. My glimpse was only brief, but sufficient for me to recognise the proud slender form of Mrs Torrence standing perfectly motionless in the silence. Completely static, as static as an image etched into the ether, yet filled with watchful ... malignancy?
Remembering her first effusive greeting I found this hard to believe; yet my nerve had left

111

me, with all wish at that hour to proceed further. I paused until the figure was withdrawn, swallowed up once more by the encompassing shadows of earth and air that wreathed fitfully about the building, subsiding again into a steady drift of thin wind-blown rain.

Then, reluctantly, but at the same time suddenly released from strain, I hurried back the way I had come, wet leaves and twigs brushing my face intermittently, with the sad sighing of the elements rustling and whining through the sparse trees.

I spent that evening in the bar of the hostelry, making myself as sociable as possible with the natives, in an effort to glean information concerning the Torrence household.

Among other things I learned that the house was called Greywaters, that Mrs Torrence was a recluse, called herself a widow, though locals heard she'd been jilted at the altar twenty years ago, and came to the district afterwards to get over the shock.

An elderly man, a well-to-do farmer, and more communicative than the rest confided to me that he was sure it was true, as he knew folks who'd been living near to her at the time.

'Came from a place called Eastbrook, about twenty-five miles up north,' he said ruminatively. 'An only child she was, daughter of the squire there. Well over thirty when it happened; and that may have accounted for it, poor thing.'

'Why "poor thing"?' I asked.

He shrugged. 'You know how some women are when they're getting a bit past it and fancy they're on the shelf ... all dead set to catch the first unsuspecting male to come along. Well *he* came ... Harry Torrence. Interested in antiques, like her father, and she nabbed him like a cunning spider after a fat young fly. He may've been dazzled a bit, at first. She was handsome in a way, I've heard, and had money to her name. Probably he didn't see straight in the beginning being so much younger. And when he did ... well, he took to his heels in the nick of time, and that's about all.' He paused, adding almost instantly, 'Of course it was a dirty trick. The shock did for her father, and I suppose when he'd gone she'd nothing left but to dry up into bitter spinsterhood and a hatred of people ... obviously.'

Sensing that something far more explanatory might lie behind the story, I said as casually as possible, 'What about ... children? Was she by any chance pregnant?'

I thought his glance at me sharpened, before he answered more definitely than was necessary, 'Oh *no*. Certainly not *that*. Esther Carruthers wasn't the type of woman to fall into a sexual trap. Very proud, and clever enough to retain woman's deadliest weapon ... the carrot for the donkey's nose so to speak ...

113

her virginity.'

'I *see*.' But I certainly didn't.

'Why?' I heard him say. 'What made you ask?'

'I saw a girl there when I called yesterday,' I told him. 'She was introduced by Mrs Torrence ... I mean Miss Carruthers ... or ...'

'Call her Mrs Torrence. Everyone does now,' the man interrupted. 'No point in reviving old issues. Well, you were saying?'

'The girl was introduced to me as Iris, her daughter,' I told him flatly. 'And it seems strange she'd have said so if she wasn't.'

'Hm.'

I waited for a further show of interest, for more information. There was none. But after a pause my companion went on, 'Leave matters as they are, and don't go there. That's my advice. I have it on good authority there's no daughter. The girl you saw may have been the child of a servant; quite likely you know.'

'You mean adopted?'

He shook his head. 'No. Not exactly. But, as I've said, Esther Torrence is a strange woman. And one thing I *do* know. She doesn't like visitors, especially at ...'

'*Sunset?*' I interjected sharply.

I fancied he was taken aback. He looked away abruptly for a moment, then said with a complete change of mood, 'Come come, sir. This talk's unnecessary, and not really very interesting. What about another pint?'

114

Knowing I should get nothing more out of him that night, I agreed. But the next morning I set off again for Greywaters.

The weather had changed again, and was windless, with quiet sunlight flooding the landscape to serenity. I walked smartly, forcing myself into a practical mood, determined this time not to be deterred by any hostile glances or frigid comments from 'the lady of the manor' as I now thought of her. After all, she had indicated at the beginning of our first meeting that I 'must call again', which was just what I was doing ... while observing her statement concerning the 'sunset' hour.

Eleven a.m. was surely a reasonable time to call, the period when most people with the leisure took coffee or a drink of some kind. I might be considered to be cashing in on the fact, but it didn't bother me. All I wished was to have the chance of meeting Iris again.

So whistling faintly to myself—a habit I had when extra courage was needed—I went boldly through the gate and copse, walking quickly up the path bordering the lawn, to the front door. I was about to pull the iron bell, when movement behind the right window caught my attention. I looked to the glass, and through the fitful light of pale sunshine and shadow, saw the curtains parted a fraction more than they had been, with a long white hand holding them in position. For a brief few seconds I was aware, too, of burning dark eyes turned upon

115

me watchfully. The face was pale, withdrawn, but I knew whose it was, though the features were blurred by reflected light. The impact on my nerves was immediate, I could feel my heart hammering and a choking feeling in the throat, at the same time deriding myself for such a stupid reaction.

Merely a *woman*; a mother possessing an irrational interest in her daughter's friends, I told myself stubbornly, and was about to turn to the bell-pull again, when the door opened, revealing the sturdy form of the woman I'd seen previously carrying the tea things away.

She glanced at me questioningly, her small mouth pulled into downward lines, button eyes cold beneath frowning brows.

'Yes?'

'I ... I would like to speak to Mrs Torrence, if you don't mind,' I said, after a pause that seemed interminable ... there was something so calculating, so hostile, almost reptilian in her look, it gave the unpleasant chill feeling of a snake about to strike, although her body certainly had nothing of a snake's grace.

'You can't,' she said in flat uncompromising tones. 'The mistress sees no one at this time of the day. You should make enquiries before you call.'

She was about to shut the door in my face when I forestalled the rebuff by placing my foot firmly over the step.

'Miss Iris then?' I persisted. 'I don't want to

be a nuisance, but I take it *Miss* Torrence is allowed to meet friends occasionally?'

For a moment the woman appeared taken aback, then she replied, as a dull red suffused her face, 'Miss Iris isn't here.'

'Not *here*? But...'

'She's out.' How glibly the lie fell I thought, and what a fool she must take me for.

'Oh, I see. Very well, I'll wait.' Adding quickly, 'Oh ... you needn't ask me *in*. I can wander about the garden or the lanes for a bit. I suppose she *will* return eventually.'

My unconscious blackmail paid off. The next moment a door in the hall clicked open, and the tall commanding figure of Mrs Torrence appeared from the shadows. It is hard to describe now, the peculiar menace I sensed emanating from her form, a power not so much physical as mental, a concentrated mental force without emotion or feeling, that drained resistance from me, leaving me chilled and static under her imperious stare. I wanted to reason and argue with her, to demand some explanation for my strange reception. But I had no line to go upon, no logical cause for complaint, since I had merely called, apparently, at an inconvenient time, and she had a perfect right to forbid my entrance. Yet what had I done that was wrong, I wondered, to set the household against me, when she had seemed at our initial first meeting to be for a few minutes so friendly and anxious for me to shake hands with Iris?

Standing there for that awkward period of time I recalled with sudden distaste the soft touch of her own velvety grey kid gloves, followed by the pleasurable impact of the girl's fragile fingers under my own. I knew then there was something wrong, something certainly 'not right' between them, a conviction endorsed by the thin cold voice saying, 'Please do not come again. My daughter is delicate and rests for most of the day. That you appeared before at her brief leisure period ... was unfortunate ... for us. I tried to make you welcome, for Iris's sake. But you should have left immediately. I told you, didn't I, at sunset she always retires, and morning visitors are barred.'

'Then some afternoon, earlier?'

'I said do *not come again*,' she reiterated. 'Do you understand?'

'No. I ...'

What I was going to add I never knew myself, because at that point the door was slammed firmly in my face.

Clenching my fists at my sides in angry frustration, tinged with uneasy fear, I turned, and went dejectedly back to the lane. From the distance the peacocks were screaming through the quiet air, and the undergrowth was bright and steaming under a thin haze of lifting mist. Bushes and the pale fronds of young curling ferns glimmered brightly from the spangled filaments of spiders webs, and as I walked down the lane all the sweetness and beauty of young summer were resolved, in imagination, into one face, one form ... that of a haunting ethereal looking girl, who just for a few instants had crossed my path, or rather I hers, and then disappeared it seemed for ever.

But why? Why? There was nothing particularly repulsive or ineligible about me I hoped. I wasn't bad-looking, uneducated, or of poor family, which should have been obvious to a keen observer like 'Madam' Torrence; and I certainly could not be accused, in country terms, of wanting to court the girl, as I didn't know her.

The whole thing, in retrospect, seemed ridiculous. And yet I knew it wasn't; knew that behind the innocent looking facade of Greywaters there lurked a mystery too intriguing to ignore. Clearly there was no point in returning to the house by daylight when I should probably be seen and dismissed more curtly than before. There might even be a man-servant about the premises ready for a down-to-earth physical challenge which I certainly didn't want. The choice left to me was to go there either at nightfall or in the early morning when it was still dark, and I decided on the latter, although even then I couldn't see what the visit would achieve, beyond giving a clearer lie of the land, and a chance to examine the back of the building, and surrounding terrain.

Luckily for me the following day was fine but overcast, which meant that when I set off at six-ish there was no risk of premature daylight revealing my intrusion. Naturally when I went out by the side door of the inn 'mine host', who was about earlier than usual, threw me a perplexed glance.

'Couldn't you sleep then, sir?' he enquired. 'The girl's just about to take up the tea.'

'Oh, tell her not to bother about mine,' I answered equably. 'And I had a very good night indeed. I just felt like a legstretch before breakfast. Good for the appetite. I often go for a mile or so at this time. Keeps you fit.'

'Hm.'

Whether he believed me or not I didn't know. Probably the latter, which would have been quite correct. In the usual way of things only wild horses could have dragged me out of bed before eight, especially at college where late-night affairs were apt to make one obnoxiously sleepy in the mornings.

However, *hoping* I'd fooled him, because I'd guessed by then both the man and his wife sensed I was up to something—something concerning Greywaters—and wanting to keep the matter to myself, I pushed off before he'd time to throw out any intimidating questions, and was soon nearing the bend at the bottom of the hill.

By then the dark silhouetted trees and bushes were faintly discernible through the grey air, but only as massed shapes against slightly paler tones of uniformity. Behind the house, when I got there, a dim streak of dawn was lifting above the horizon, but furred and indefinite like the wan light of a stage-set penetrating a thick gauze curtain. The smell of mist was heavy and odorous with the tang of wet earth and growing verbage, stagnant almost; suggestive of half dead things struggling for life. A queer place and no mistake. As before, when I pushed through the spinney to the garden I had the odd, unreal sensation of animation suspended out of time ... of wandering beyond human habitat to spheres unknown. There was even an element of brooding, creeping danger, that stiffened me to chilled caution, impelling a wariness of tread, of proceeding always in the inky shadows, pausing for a few moments as a light appeared briefly, furred and misted at an upstairs window, then as quickly disappeared.

The housekeeper, I thought as I went on again, or one of the servants. I'd not counted on such an eventuality, forgotten in my keenness to investigate that *someone* was sure to be about at such an hour. This meant extra care. To be caught out like any trespassing schoolboy could mean not only trouble for myself, but a foiling of all my plans.

The light was gradually lifting. But with it, to my great relief, a thickening of the early mist. When I reached the side of the house, nothing, thankfully, was really visible except the looming dark structure of walls and hooded windows, of bleak dripping glass further on, obviously that of a conservatory or large greenhouse. The former, I guessed, since a wan light penetrated from its interior to the gravel path, as though heating or some form of radiation had been left on, possibly to encourage hot-house plants. All such conjectures were vague in my mind, but sufficiently compelling to take me there, padding silently, slowly and half on tip-toe, crouched against the wall like some furtive animal aware of danger yet unable to resist the challenge of ... what?

I pressed on until my face came suddenly against the cold impact of glass.

And then ... I saw it.

The stiff figure of a woman that I took at first to be some effigy, seated rigidly on a wooden bench, staring ahead, glassy-eyed, and apparently without life, towards the conglomeration of plants and succulent creepers at the far end of the interior. A queer luminous light exuded from her form, intensifying for a second, fading, then deepening again, quivering into the semblance of a distorted form, before it once more subsided into negation. Horrified, I watched the mask of face—Esther Torrence's—tremble into chattering mobility as the pale lips formed one word, calling, it seemed, the dead or the unborn, to life ... 'Iris ... Iris ...' The whisper vibrated through the silence, shivering the leaves, penetrating the glass frames in a shudder of wind before the eerie aura of the woman's body curdled and resolved itself towards an ethereal developing feminine figure materialising every second more firmly into that of the girl I had met on the lawn ... the lovely Iris whose delicate hand had lain so briefly in mine, and who had been so ruthlessly banished at the moment of sunset.

With my knees shaking, but supporting myself against the wooden frame and wall, I retained sufficient clarity of mind to watch her approach her 'mother' ... or whatever she was, on faltering uncertain steps. By then I could actually *see* the rise and fall of the pathetic young creature's breast, hear mentally, if not physically, that one supplicatory word 'Mama' ... as the fragile lips opened and shut with the gesture of a robot.

Then Mrs Torrence rose from her seat, tall, majestic, and intensely horrifying as she lifted one angular arm, gloved from the elbow, and with a curious malicious power, ordered the girl to sit. Helplessly Iris, or that which I knew *as* Iris, obeyed and seated herself at the far end of the bench, becoming each second that passed, more identifiable in human shape ... a shivering terrified elemental creature conjured up by no natural process of birth, but from the insatiable repressed power of one crazy

123

woman's lust to possess and command.

Yes. I knew it.

There was no mystery any more except of the evil concentration cultivated through years of hatred and suppressed sexual and spiritual frustration. A concentration so intense it had enabled Esther Torrence, at last, to create from an extension of her own will a replica of life sufficiently realistic to satisfy her own lusting ego. The mere thought of the long hours spent each day kindling matter from thought ... the etheric image from obscene mental greed ... not only terrified, but disgusted me. Did others, any who had the chance, see as I saw, I wondered? The housekeeper? The woman I'd watched carrying a tray over the lawn that afternoon, just before sunset?

'Just before sunset'. The phrase hit me with fresh impact as I recalled my sudden dismissal from Greywaters, and the old man's previous warning.

'Not theer,' he'd said. 'Never at sunset.'

I knew now, why. Sunset meant disintegration of 'Iris's' brief existence in the real world. Sometime, somehow, perhaps a local or chance passer-by like myself had been unwitting witness to the haunting scene—the mirage, ghost, or whatever it was, as daylight finally died into evening, leaving Esther Torrence bereft until hours of baleful dedication brought fulfilment again. Word had got out, therefore, of strange happenings at

Greywaters, which no one round about wished to probe.

And as I walked through the grey morning to the lane I almost wished I hadn't, knowing that what I'd seen was not only macabre, but unholy.

Hurrying down the hill to the pub, I wondered for how many minutes of each day Mrs Torrence was able to indulge her satisfaction, and how long under such intense strain, she herself would endure.

I did not have to wait long for an answer.

Shortly after my return to university that autumn, I saw in a brief newspaper paragraph that the dead body of a woman known as Mrs Torrence had been found in an emaciated state in the conservatory of a lonely house near the Cornish border.

For many years Mrs Torrence had been known as an eccentric, and during the last few months her household staff had left, leaving her to live alone. She had obviously not eaten for a considerable time, and strewn about the garden were also the corpses of several peacocks. A curious feature of the case is that a strand of light brown hair like that of a child or young girl's, was clutched in one of the dead woman's gloved hands, and at first it was thought she might have had company at the time of her decease. This however has been disproved by the authorities. No suggestion of foul play is suspected.

I knew that of course, realised also that the only foul play in the affair had been that of her own making. Although I have never been conventionally religious, I *do* believe there are boundaries between the known and unknown which should not be tampered with. Possibly Esther Torrence knows it now, too. Although I doubt it.

CHAPTER SEVEN

POOR JOE

As he cut down the hill from the brightness of the moor towards the village, a creeping sense of dismay filled him. The nearer he approached, the more desolate the place appeared, with lingering drifts of snow still straggling thinly towards the main street. The cottages, greyish-white, appeared squat and small, the square bereft of life, except for a goods van moving slowly past the church, a woman wearing a headscarf dragging a small child into the post-office, and an old man with a sack on his back.

He remembered it of course. He'd been born and bred there, worked as a tinner in the mine until better prospects had called him to the States. Done well, too. But he'd wanted to return for a break, take up with his folk and childhood acquaintances again for old times' sake. Not that he was old yet, not by a long chalk. In his youthful prime you could say. And as he passed his hand over his thatch of crisp curls he envisaged his parents' pleasure and pride when he appeared.

The walk from the station had been a long one though, and he was more tired than he thought. Perhaps that accounted for the drab look of things. Well ... drab was an understatement. A ghost place it appeared, with grey forms shuffling against the darker greyness of buildings and deepening shadows. How could it have changed so much in such a comparatively short time? When he'd left there'd have been men tramping their ways home from the day shift at the mine at such an hour, and the hillside on a fine day would have rung with the Bal Maidens singing.

Now, as he passed the first few straggling cottages there was nothing. Nothing but the quietness of inaction and slow decay.

He shivered, with a chill dread freezing his spine. On the rim of the opposite hill beyond the church and far end of the village, a mine-stack stood bleak and dark with no rhythmic motion of pumping rod against the leaden sky.

Where had the sun gone?

He stood motionless for a moment lured by an almost irresistible impulse to turn back, leaving the past to memory and bygone things. But the thought of his mother checked him.

She'd believed in him always, and he wanted to show her what a fine upstanding young fellow he'd become, with money in his pocket too. A failure the others had thought him; nothing but a dreamer, lacking the grit or commonsense to keep up with his fellow workers—a 'Johnny-head-in-the-air' all bombast and fine talk.

Fine talk was it?

He'd show them.

So he strode on, down the cobbled street, which had a few folk about now, but none he knew. He searched for a familiar face, keeping his eyes skinned and senses alert; there was no one. No one at all, only the darkening light over the lingering remains of snow, and the icy chill seeping through his bones. The Ancient Goat wasn't yet open, or he'd have gone in for a drink. Pubs were matey places. Someone there would be sure to recognise him and call ... 'Well well! ef tedn' Joe Carn. Come in, lad, come in and have a dram wi' us. You'm lookin' real handsome. Good to see 'ee 'tes, an' that's for sure.'

Yes, it would be something like that, warm and cheering to waken the heart in him again.

But as he passed the building towards the side street where his family lived, the foreboding he'd felt on the hill returned, increasing to queer unreasoning panic. For the first time he felt an alien, outcast, wandering almost in another sphere of time. The houses of the ancient place seemed to converge and lean towards him, blank eyes staring, doors closed and secretive against the elements. All the memories he'd had were sucked away by the greedy covetousness of place, whispering and sneering as though in condemnation.

A burly man wearing a fisherman's jersey bumped into him round the corner, continuing on his way as though he wasn't really there. Joe

129

paused, staring after him as the large figure was swallowed up by the shadows and disappeared.

Then he knew.

Knew that this place he'd come to wasn't a real place any more, but something projected from his own mind taking on a miserable semblance of the village he'd known as a boy.

A ghost town, without substance or life, harbouring not flesh and blood people, but ghosts.

A kind of nausea rose in him. He had a great longing to turn and cut up the hill again to the bright moorland he'd left behind.

But it was too late.

As he paused uncertainly he saw the bent figure of an aged woman turn from a doorway moving slowly, awkwardly, in his direction. She must have been well on into the eighties, but something about her struck a familiar cord, and puzzled him until the moment of meeting, when the truth with a tremendous shock registered.

The fine nose was the same, the old eyes still blue in their wrinkled sockets; but the mouth that had once always seemed to quiver on the brink of laughter or tears was drawn in networked lines towards her chin. The once firm breasts sagged beneath the bent back. Grey hair straggled where gold had formerly been.

'Mother...' he whispered, with a hand outstretched, but she neither saw nor heard,

130

simply pressed on, passing through him as easily as a puff of wind down the street.

Automatically he lifted his fingers to his face, and found there . . . nothing.

He would have turned then and climbed the incline to the summit of the hill. But there was no need.

A sudden gust of air caught and carried him more easily than a dead leaf higher and higher into the air, until he became one with the moor and the heather above . . . a mere sigh among all the other sighings of the cold evening; the ghost of a man who fifty years before had left for foreign parts. The next day his body was found frozen in a ditch not far from the station.

No one would have recognised him, and his mother when she heard, did not entirely understand. She merely shook her head murmuring, 'Poor Joe. Poor Joe.' After all, it was so very long ago.

CHAPTER EIGHT

THE MAY TREE

This morning when I woke up I felt my hand. Would you believe it, there was another one there? A knobbly hard lump of a thing just below my thumb, looking exactly like one of those notches on the old May tree at the bottom of my garden. I was rather intrigued by then; there were so many of them appearing where most humans don't have them ... quite painless, and covered with a sort of bark. Amusing in a macabre lurid kind of way.

Of course, the May tree *was* very ancient and when we first took the cottage Wikksvale, I'd thought of having it cut down ... Sally, my young wife, wanted me to, because she said it looked nasty in some lights, especially our first days there in the winter, with no leaves on, or green to brighten its twisted limbs. That's what she said, 'limbs' instead of branches, which seems odd now, when I come to write everything down. You see I'm trying to record things exactly as they were, in view of later events which may prove interesting to historians and geologists.

I must admit I wasn't impressed favourably myself, and had half a mind to tackle the job on my own before the spring came, but with the cottage still needing so much renovating and painting up to get it really comfortable and cosy to live in, I let time slip by, and by April when the blossom was appearing I just hadn't the heart to.

Why should an old thing be destroyed, I thought, when it still had the capacity to flower and shake its petals in the wind? The idea, from such an angle, seemed desecration, partly perhaps because of my environmental post, which meant taking a two year intensive survey of the district ... both from naturalistic and future planning possibilities.

I assumed that with the brighter weather Sally would feel the same; she'd always been an enthusiastic country-lover, and although the nearest village was Tallack, almost a mile away, we weren't exactly cut off. There was a farm on the moors over the high lane, a short walk up the slope, and a cottage or two scattered about. But as the days lengthened she seemed gradually to take an aversion to Wikksvale.

'There's something unpleasant about it,' she said one evening as dying sunlight was merging quietly into greenish twilight, leaving just a rim of rosy gold behind. 'Cooped up.'

'What do you mean, cooped up? Good heavens, after that cramped London flat...'

'It's not that. Not the *size*. The atmosphere, I think. The *oldness*. And it's not only the cottage ... the whole *place*, John. Especially that tree...' She wandered to the window overlooking the garden where a white froth of bloom foamed almost luminously over a brook splashing to a quiet overhung pool.

I was at a loss, and a bit irritated, because Sally, though sensitive, was normally a rational young woman, with a keen sense of artistic beauty.

'Can't you forget the tree for a few minutes in the day?' I said with an edge to my voice. 'What's wrong with it, for Pete's sake? Decorative I call it. A real natural asset.'

'Well, I don't,' she retorted sharply. 'And if you must know, I wish we'd never come here. I wish we could leave and find some other house to live.'

'Then you'll just have to go on wishing, my love,' I told her firmly. 'If you had any *reason* ... if the plumbing was bad, or the inside damp, or the water supply wrong ... well then, I'd agree. But there's not a damn thing to complain about, practically, now is there?'

'Oh no. Not *practically*,' Sally answered. 'That's just it.'

'What do you mean?'

She turned and came back to me, lifting her violet-grey eyes to mine with the maddening pleading look in them that had generally got her way in the past. Then she said, 'John ... darling ... tell me, haven't *you* felt it?'

'What?'

'It's not *ours*. We've bought it, yes. But there

135

are some things no one can buy. The past ... or something left over that remains. You've felt it too, haven't you ... *haven't* you?'

'Sally, I don't ...'

'Yes, you do understand,' she insisted before I could finish. 'You know you do. I've watched you sometimes when it's quiet and there's no wind. *Listening.* What do you listen for, John? And what is it you see when the shadows come ... or haven't you found it yet?'

'What on earth are you talking about?'

She shrugged, a helpless gesture, and turned away. 'I don't know. If I did, it would be easier. Or even if you'd confide in me. Why won't you?'

'Because you're talking nonsense,' I said. 'There's simply nothing to tell you, except ...'

'Yes? *Except?*'

'The quietness. That's all. Who was it said there was no such thing as complete silence? Some writing Johnny or other. Well it's true enough. Everywhere there are vibrations, stirring of leaves and wind, little animals nosing about outside, the creak of a floorboard, old wood shrinking ...'

'Don't.' Sally's voice was shrill and loud.

I stared at her. '*Now* what? I was only explaining.'

'I know, I know.' A little of the sudden fear left her face as she resumed more quietly, 'Old wood shrinking, it's a horrible term to use. Like that thing in the garden ...'

'What thing?' I tried to sound casual, although I knew very well what she meant.

'The tree. It should be cut.'

'Ah well...' I prevaricated, 'when these flowers die perhaps, but not in full bloom, Sally. And *you* shouldn't want that either ... being such a ballet lover.'

'What do you mean?' Her tones were so intimidating I was caught momentarily off my guard.

'Haven't you noticed how it frills out sometimes ... like a girl's skirt ... a ballerina's?' I said, 'Old it may be. But at odd moments ... God! I think I've never seen anything more beautiful, especially in the evenings and early mornings before it's quite light...'

'So *that's* what you're doing when you sneak about in the early hours, watching *her*. That's what you're listening to when the stairs creak, waiting for her to come down, and don't think I haven't *seen*. I've seen too much already; a thin face with sly dark eyes and black hair, and a way of moving her snaky arms that's horrible ... just *horrible*.'

I was really perturbed then.

'Look, honey,' I said, putting my arm round her, 'please, *please*. You've seen nothing, *heard* nothing. Except what's in your own head. Do you think it's because you're ... are you ...?'

She pulled herself away abruptly. 'No. I'm not pregnant. I wish I was. But I never will be

137

... here.'

'Sally, sweetheart ...'

She had her back to me then and was staring out of the window. I thought what a graceful back it was, as she lifted one delicately formed arm to her face, with a screwed up handkerchief in the hand; erect and slim, gently flowing from a small waist and swelling thighs to tapering calves and ankles. Her hair was gold ... the dusky muted gold of amber flooded by warm sunlight. I wanted her suddenly with an aching love that longed to comfort and lull her into forgetfulness of everything but myself. So I lifted her up, and carried her to our room, putting her gently on the bed, where she lay with a haunted longing look in her enormous eyes.

I didn't have to say anything more. But when loving was over and we were at peace, I noticed the trace of tears on the lovely contours of her cheek bones. Tracing a finger there, I said, 'Sally ... love ...'

'Sh ... shsh ...!' she shook her head slowly, then laid her face against my shoulder, whispering, 'I was being stupid. There was nothing, John, nothing at all. Imagination, just as you said. That's all it was.'

But I was not convinced.

And as the days passed a haunting feeling grew in me that Sally might be right. Unlike her, though, I was not perturbed, merely interested, and though I wouldn't admit it, fascinated by the sense of an alien presence felt, but not physically seen at the beginning ... and by an insidious drift of perfume lingering on the air, in hall, stairs, or by the kitchen, as a soft wind from the garden seeped through cracks, or with a sudden flurry from any open windows or doors.

There were times too, when I fancied a watchful figure lurked in the shadows, and I recalled Sally's description of a thin face framed by black hair; envisaged her so strongly that at odd moments I could actually glimpse movement, and as I waited heard—or *thought* I heard—the distant echo of mocking laughter.

This was generally in the evenings, and when I looked out across the garden the transient light would give the queer semblance of a flying, dancing, shadowy creature whirling into the film of rising mist near the pool and ancient May tree.

Of course I never divulged it to my wife. And as spring lengthened into summer, Sally's resentment was less obvious, though she appeared pre-occupied and rather silent, and many times I found her wandering alone to the pool, where she'd stand abstractedly looking first into the water, then at the tree.

Once, putting my arm round her waist from behind I said, 'Glad you're getting used to things now, Sally.'

She gave a little jerk, turning quickly.

'Oh. You startled me. I wish you wouldn't.'

'What do you mean? I can't help it if you don't hear.'

'You walk so softly.'

I laughed.

'It's the grass.'

She shook her head.

'No. You always seem to appear when ... when...'

'Yes?'

She didn't answer my question, just put her hand to her lips saying, 'Listen.'

Trying to match her mood, I waited for a few moments with my ears alert, and although I told myself it was mere imagination, it *did* seem the earth pulsed and murmured in a muted half-legible way, sighing, calling, soughing seductively through the grass, rippling over the pool and shining water-weeds to the old May which was green and brown now, with the blossom fallen, and only a last few petals scattering the ground below.

I jerked myself into answering reasoningly, 'Summer, Sally. Just the summer calling...'

She shrugged, turned quickly as though my remark had angered her and started back to the house, saying, 'If it is, I'd rather have the sound of cars and traffic round me. Why couldn't you have a got a post nearer civilization? Why can't you *now*? It's not too late, is it?'

'Yes,' I told her shortly. 'We're here, and I'm not being driven from a good job and a perfectly satisfactory home, simply because of a ... a *mood*.'

'Why don't you say neurosis and have done with it,' my wife retorted bitterly. 'Or do you think I need a psychoanalyst? Is that it?'

'Perhaps,' I agreed nastily, thinking this might very well be true, and trying at the same time to dispel the uncomfortable experience I'd undergone myself a moment or two before.

She didn't reply, and presently trying to be conciliatory, I said, 'Come on, snap out of it. Why spoil a nice summer day by useless bickering?'

'Nice?' she said coldly, with a maddening refusal to be appeased. 'If you think so, I suppose it's all right.'

Ignoring the sarcasm, I went to my small cubbyhole we'd nicknamed 'the study', when we first moved in. But during the months that followed it had become more of a retreat from Sally's moods than anything else. Here, at least, she seldom trespassed, and within its quiet subdued interior furnished in muted fawns and brown with only a table, cupboard, chairs and books along one wall, I could generally recover any lost equanimity to some sort of peace.

That day though was different. Although I thumbed through some of my notes and made an effort to locate certain historical details of the district, I couldn't concentrate. Something ... from outside ... or within the very precincts of the cottage itself ... seemed to linger and

141

wait, and haunt the atmosphere; a restless beguiling presence disturbing each fresh trend of thought with its implication, Sally's suggestion, of a thin pale face, dark-eyed, surrounded by a mass of tumbled black hair.

Once or twice I looked up, expecting to see her there, by the window or door, sensing instinctively what her mission was—to draw me provokingly to the garden where the May tree waited, a symbol of some unknown secret challenge, daring, yet defying me, if you like, to have it cut down.

As the days passed I knew I never would. On many occasions, when Sally was out at the village shopping, or upstairs resting, I'd take my hatchet, ready to start the job. But when I got there, something about the twisted form with its yellowing tired leaves and naked arms forbade me, and I'd turn away, hearing a shiver of relief about the terrain, or a woman's sigh . . . I don't know; it's hard to explain the disturbing conflict of mind and heart that assailed me at each time of confrontation. And harder still to express in words the growing conviction that the apparition, only half defined as yet, and the tree were one. But that's how it was.

And Sally knew it.

Although, when autumn came, she never referred to the old May any more, her brooding tortured eyes, tightened lips, and half fearful glance behind her shoulder when she thought I was not looking, told me her mind was completely possessed, and that the routine of cooking, cleaning, and attending to our mutual needs, were merely automatic responses to habit. Her thoughts, if any, were elsewhere.

I should, of course, have seen that she went to a doctor. Perhaps have given in to her wish to move and taken a house elsewhere. There *were* places going, nearer the hamlet, which might have satisfied her. Most men probably would have done so. But by then I myself had trespassed, or been taken ... beyond the realms of commonsense and in my own way, but more pleasantly than Sally, had become as much a slave to the atmosphere as she was.

Anyway, September passed into early October, with mists hugging the landscape, creeping insidiously from the distant sea, or high hills on the west, which in the evenings sometimes seemed to loom closer, like the forms of great primeval beasts waking slowly from slumber. For days on end, the moors were quiet and undistinguishable under thickening veils of yellowing light which left a damp earthy odour on the air, seeping even into the kitchen and sitting-room where log fires burned.

Sally's silent presence began to oppress me. There were moments even when a slow heavy rage burned in me. Periods of violent reaction when a voice seemed to whisper in my ear; 'Get rid of her ... kill her ... send her away ... kill

143

her ... kill her ...'

Then I'd recover, and trembling, filled with remorse, would fortify myself with a stiff drink, and try to make up to my wife with love.

But Sally no longer wanted loving or affection from me. All she wanted, and I knew this, though she never said so any more, was to be away.

And in the middle of November she went.

Just disappeared one afternoon when I was struggling with some notes in the study, and never came back. I thought at first she might have taken a trip from the village to Pornallen five miles from there, where there were some good shops. But when I enquired later I was told the last bus had returned and Sally certainly wasn't on it. I reported the case to the police, as a matter of routine, but there again, came to a dead end. And what a simile to use, under the circumstances.

Apt though, as things turned out.

Of course I should have felt grief, but as this is a truthful document, as truthful as I can make it, I must admit that my only reaction was one of relief. Without Sally I was able to indulge any whim or fancy I chose. For the first time since my marriage I was free ... and like the tree ... out of danger and able to be myself.

The strange thing was, that although those dark winter days should have been inducive to work and study they didn't react on me in this way at all. To the contrary, most of my time, except for walks to the farm where I obtained most of my provisions, was spent idly wandering about the house or doing a bit of digging and tidying in the garden. 'You should have been a horticulturalist, old chap,' I found myself saying aloud one day, as I hacked some weeds from the base of the old May, and then laughed uneasily, aware I'd done rather a lot of it lately, chatting at odd moments to some other 'me' that existed outside the physical body of John Markham, to someone or 'thing' that was starting to intrude even upon my material image.

Yes. It was about then that I began to notice the lumps; those curious bark-like protuberances which appeared from time to time on my form quite without warning, generally in the mornings following a night's sleep, when I woke up, and stretched myself, creaking a little as though the pangs of rheumatism were attacking me. There was no pain though, and when I was dressed and about I'd feel oddly jaunty and ready to face an active day with spade and fork about my domain. In the evenings it was different. I was content then to relax by a blazing log fire in the sitting room, and ruminate about nothing in particular until I fell into a comforting doze, and stayed there until it was time for bed.

Sometimes I didn't bother to go upstairs. There was no point really. It was easier to remain where I was, listening to the wind

145

moaning outside, and the beating of twigs on the window. And the lamplight then was more companionable than the complete dark. I suppose when I look back now, I was secretly a little afraid of the 'thing' I'd created, the environment of 'aloneness' that was in itself an invitation to that other one—the indigenous 'familiar' of the wanton wild terrain—eyes that were pools of night, and black blown hair as errant as the raven's wing. Occasionally I'd feel a soft touch on my shoulder, and look round startled, expecting to glimpse her briefly, with the taunting smile on her lips, which though sensed, I'd never seen. The lamp would flicker for a second, and I'd catch the half materialised vision of a face ... hear the soft flurry of footsteps and blown skirts as the wind stirred the rug on the floor. Then it was over. There'd be only the firelight sending contorted shadows up the walls, only my own hands stretched before me to the blaze, with most probably another knot on them, at the wrist perhaps, or further up the arm, near the elbow.

In early January I had more than a dozen on all parts of my body. There was one at my temple, another near the nose, which I tried to hide by growing a beard and whiskers. The farmer and his family began to eye me strangely. Once the wife said with a hint of apology mingled with—was it revulsion in her voice?—'Don't you think you should see a doctor, sir? Or ... or perhaps leave that place?'

'Why?' I said lightly, though I knew only too well. 'I'm quite fit ... except for a touch of rheumatism here and there. In the spring when the warmer weather comes it will all clear up.'

But it didn't.

And I was careful by then to let no one see me face to face, arranging with the farm boy to deliver what food I required and leave it in a bin put specially outside my door for me to take in when I was certain no one was about.

Oh yes. To most normal human beings it must have seemed a strange withdrawn life I led then. But I was completely satisfied with my own company, and that of my unseen companion who whispered in my ears at odd times when least expected ... 'Come along ... come out with me. It's cold there, but dark and quiet and filled with secrets ...'

Did she really speak I wonder now? Or was it merely her mind communing through my inner ear ... the ear of my unknown self ... of waving tree and bark and wind, of the deep earth from which all life springs?

I'm saying this so that any of you who may one day read these notes will not think my experience all bad. Indeed goodness and badness, as rational individuals of the everyday world see them, simply don't exist for me any more.

I am what I am ... a creature hour by hour, day by day, drawn ever nearer its natural habitat; and this evening as the first pale rays of a winter moon light the deep green dusk, I shall steal out and become one with the force that calls ... forever calls from that ancient May.

As I said, at the very beginning, when I woke up this morning there was another one there, a knobbly hard lump of a thing just below my thumb, and as the minutes tick towards afternoon they are developing in increasing numbers.

I have turned the hall glass to the wall, in case I should inadvertently have a glimpse of myself when passing. Stupid really, because I can well imagine it—encrusted face and thickened twigs of hair like those of an old tree reaching for air. Not pleasant by human standards, but intensely interesting to an analytical mind.

Oh yes. My mind so far, is free to explore and range through numerous spheres of thought and experience.

In a little while perhaps ...? But then why envisage a future when the present is so completely and diversely absorbing?

The light at last is certainly darkening; and the air seeping into the cottage from the garden, heavy with the odour and colour of deep fungoid yellow. Note my actions now. I get up from the chair, take up this document, and with a somewhat staggering lumbering gait make my way down the hall through the kitchen and back door to the garden and the old May.

There is a trowel ready, waiting at the foot of the twisted trunk. I knew I should want it ... though *how* I knew I can't tell you.

I kneel down and start using it, towards ... a twisted dirt-grimed hand, more of a claw really, groping through the soil and stones, and behind it a hag's face, half eaten or blackened by peat and fire, smothered in cobwebs and grime ... but *moving* ... pushing towards me, with broken hungry fangs of teeth and reddened orbs that leer and glow as the gnarled root-fingers stretch and clutch ... seeking my neck ... snaking and entwining until ... until ... it's true, remember. *All true.*

* * *

Extract from local paper.

'A macabre discovery was made yesterday afternoon during police investigations concerning the disappearance of John Markham, a surveyor, when his body was found half submerged, with indications of strangulation, at the base of a May tree bordering the property Wikksvale, not far from Tallack.

'Further digging on the site revealed also the remains of a woman, thought to be his wife, more deeply interred. A curious feature of both is that the roots of the tree, an exceedingly ancient one, should so completely have entangled the two corpses, with disfiguring results.

'Until Mr Markham took the place a year ago, the property had been untenanted for a considerable period, due probably to its reputation of being haunted by the spirit of a woman burned as a witch there in the seventeenth century. According to legend and ancient annals of the district, Agnes Penluvass, a young woman of great beauty was said to have the powers of casting spells, and ensnaring any man she fancied to her home, after which he was never seen again.

'Following police findings a coroner's inquest will be held, a suggestion being that Markham himself may have disposed first of his wife, then at a later date have taken his own life, although so far there is no proof of this.

'A farmer living nearby said that for many months Markham had been acting strangely, and latterly had lived the life of a recluse. On the rare occasions he had been seen outside the house, his face and hands had appeared swathed in bandage, but when a doctor had been sent for, he had barred and locked himself inside the cottage refusing to be seen.

'A document was found clenched in the dead man's hand, which will be thoroughly analysed before the contents are disclosed.'

CHAPTER NINE

SNOW BALLET

In the spring, when the streams trickled gently over the stones, and the thin crying of lambs came from the fields where the primroses grew, the old man was quiet, and would sit contentedly for hours by the door of the farm house, watching the hens cluck in the yard, pushing baccy into his pipe, and flapping at the flies with his cap. But when the snow fell in soft flakes against the windows and the crows were black against the white landscape, something changed in him; and as the farm cart wound like a dark phantom thing down the frost-bitten lane, he would say, over and over again, 'Ah—'twas in the snow she came dancing, so pretty and white, and in the snow I buried her.'

'Oh for goodness sake, father, do be quiet,' his daughter Nell would say impatiently. 'Forever droning on like that—fair maddening it is.'

He took no notice of her; he never did. She was a big-boned, square faced woman, and if the truth were known, he despised her, because she was born of his second wife, and had no beauty. The other, his first, had been different. It was of her he thought when the snow fell, though they'd been together only a year. And when the trees shook their whitened branches like feathered skirts, it was the skirts of Julie he saw, fluttering and furling as they had been at the show that night he'd first seen her with Boothby's Players.

It had been snowing then; but he had been young—a great strong black eyed fellow who could box or wrestle with any who came his way. Nothing queer about that—for Little Trevanion was the best run farm in the district, and except for the lad, he worked it himself. He was a man in the prime, and until the night he saw Julie poised high on her toes behind the footlights, he had thought he had all he wanted. But the sight of her there, so white and tiny, had stirred his heart like the fluttering wings of a bird; and in less than a month he had married her, when the snow was still white on the ground, and the black arms of the trees laced with silver in the frozen air.

For months they had been happy, while the winter gave place to spring, and new life came to the hills and fields, starring the ditches with flowers, and bringing the young corn green to the brown earth. And Julie, like a changeling creature, had been quick footed and bright about the farm, singing as blithely as the larks rising and dipping in the sky.

She had been a good wife those first months, learning the ways of a farmer's wife, always a little amused, ready to laugh with him on the slightest provocation, endearing herself to him in a hundred ways as the days passed. Her cooking, it was true, was not so good as his mother's had been. There were things about the house left undone. But such details then, had been unimportant to him, held as he was by her spell which had the elfin quality of a spring morning.

Then, as summer passed into autumn, and the trees grew stark against the yellowing skies, a restlessness had come to her, and she sang no more, but had her eyes more often than not fixed upon the moorland road winding like a ribbon to the little town below. And he knew what she was thinking. For soon the snow would come again; the lights would twinkle, and there would be the smell of beer and oranges in the hall where the plays were given, with the rattle of the curtain going up, and the exciting glitter of spangled legs. There would be shouting and laughter, and the clapping of hands, with the great Bill Boothby himself announcing the turns in his tall hat and tailed coat. And some other girl would dance on to the stage in her place, with her partner in the Harlequin suit.

He had not been able to bear the look in her eyes any more. Mocking words left his lips, gradually turning to bitter jibes, which, with the first frosts began slowly to freeze the life out of their love.

'Love-sick?' he had once said. 'Wishing yourself back with that namby chap?'

153

But she had not answered.

'You used not to be so dumb,' he had gone on, goading her. 'Not when I first knew you—all togged up in your fancy clothes.'

She had said nothing, even then. But her eyes were stricken, as though seeing him for the first time as he really was. And after that, things had been worse between them. Sometimes there were reconciliations, moments when the fury of suspicion in him melted to tenderness at the sight of her dainty form moving about the kitchen, or at the glint of tears in her eyes. But it had never lasted. Always, in the end, the jealousy had returned, poisoning their lives like a cancer at a healthy root, laying a blight upon the farm, which showed in a number of ways, as though fingers had traced there a pattern of despair.

And then, one night, it had happened. The show had come to the village with its lights and music, and she'd set off when he was having his mug of ale in the Tinners' Rest. He'd come back and found the farm empty, with the lamp burning, and a note by his supper put ready on the table. It read—'gone to see my folk. Will be back soon, Julie.'

He had felt the rage choking the breath out of him, because he knew she had once liked the dancing fellow, with his coloured suit and sleek black hair. His crazy fancy was already seeing her run to him, picturing in the years ahead, the farm alone and empty, with her gone from him, and only the sound of the wind round the walls, and the clucking of the fowls in the yard.

It was snowing outside, and the flakes fell soundlessly against the windows—white, like small ghosts on dancing feet. He had opened the door and gone out, with the cold softness driven against his face, clinging with feather fingers to the collar of his jacket, and to his brows and hair. The moon was up between the clouds, and he had taken the short way over the moors, while the jealousy froze hard in his heart, chilling his blood to hatred and despair. Between the moon-washed drifts of lightness odd patches of furze showed dark where the wind had driven the snow away; their swaying shapes had mockery in them, torturing him with the vision of that other dancer, who had once held Julie in his arms.

So when he actually saw them—when they really appeared there on the brow of the hill, close together in the frail light, she with her face up to the man's, he was not surprised. He had known.

He had not meant to kill her. But at the sight of them an overmastering frenzy to crush her rose up in him—to crush her as effectively as a snowdrop squeezed between his hands.

He had waited for a time in the shadow of a ruined mine work, watching her, as the man turned and was away with a cat's speed into the distances of moon-lit snow. And if he could have got him, he would have killed him too; for it was the man he wanted to kill. But there was a way between them. And so he waited, while she came down the slope, feather light, tripping and running, her skirts blown behind her, and her black hair loose, with a film of brightness on it, like scattered stars.

She had not seen him at first. But when he stepped from the shadows into the pale light she had stood for a second, with her hand gone quickly to her throat, the moon full on her white face. Near the shaft she stood, while he went towards her, slowly, purposefully, the hatred dark in his eyes and mind. She had backed away from him, till his hand went out, and she screamed wildly, shrill and high, as a sea-bird crying. He had not meant her to go over, but his fingers were on her shoulder, and she had fallen suddenly; fallen into the darkness, while the flakes still whirled like heartless dancers in their ballet of death.

At the inquest he had told his tale well. He had heard her scream, gone to look for her, and found her there. They had believed him. No one had ever known the truth; no one ever would. But when the snow came, it was always the same. He saw her as he had seen her first, in her white frock, like a swan about to fly.

That was a long time ago. Fifty years. He was an old man now, with rheumy eyes and a cough which rattled.

'Why don't you come to the fire?' said his daughter one day. 'It irritates me—hearing you cough like that.'

' 'Twas in the snow she came, so pretty and white,' he echoed, 'and in the snow I buried her.'

'You'll drive me mad,' said his daughter. 'The same thing all the time—on and on. What's the matter with you these days? Come and have a cup of tea now. Stir yourself.'

But he didn't want any tea. He didn't want to stir himself. He was old; why should he? Why should they bother him with tea, when the twilight was falling, and the snow drifted so prettily from the sky?

'Leave me alone,' he snapped. She was efficient, his daughter, as plain women generally are. And he had come to hate her efficiency as he hated her face.

'Oh very well,' she said sharply, annoyed. 'Have it your own way.'

Later, when her husband had gone to lock up the fowls, she put on her hat and coat, and went out to see a friend.

The old man breathed a sigh of relief. It was pleasant being alone. The room's silence slowly filled with dreams. He could sit there now without fear of being disturbed; nothing but the sound of the clock ticking, and the crackling of the fire, with the solitary crying of a wild bird from somewhere outside.

Presently he got up and went to the door. He opened it, and saw the world before him lying white and frozen in the winter light. Down the

157

path he could see the darker marks left by his daughter's footsteps; but soon, as he watched, the snow gathered and obscured them again, as beauty obscuring an unpleasant memory. And as he stood there a sense of happiness and anticipation possessed him. The fret of his life—these last nagging unfruitful days, with his daughter always at his shoulder arguing and brow-beating him in her strident voice—slipped away as though by magic, and it seemed to him that the falling flakes were cool lips pressed against his old cheeks. He did not even feel so very old, after all. A curious sensation of lightness was about him, as though it would be the easiest thing in the world to be carried away and lost forever in the drifts of feathered snow.

Without his coat, he went out into the silence, down the path, and up towards the moor. The snow thickened and whirled about him as his feet trod the crisp ground. There was no sound anywhere, nothing save the soft crunch of his own footsteps sending a powdered whiteness into the air. At the foot of the hill he waited, with his head raised. And then, from above, something took shape, quivered, and stood poised a moment or two before breaking into light and movement. And she was dancing alone on the hill top, her skirts twirling, and her hair blowing, whiter and lighter than the snow itself.

Down the path she came, with her arms

towards him; and when he was almost in reach of her, she turned again, and was running before him, leading him on, with her chin up, and her hands tossed high in the air. And he was no longer stumbling like an old man, but hurrying behind her, as though invisible reins held and drew him. And sometimes it seemed to him that she laughed gaily, as she had laughed in those first days; but her laughter was soundless now, hushed by the cloak of falling snow.

Then, on the edge of the shaft, she paused and waited, her skirts blowing, until he was beside her, with his arms out, reaching to reclaim her from the years. But his hands clutched nothing. The touch of her shoulders dissolved in his grasp, as his fingers closed upon only snow; snow that whirled and danced before his eyes, blinding him, claiming him, until there was a slipping of his feet, a quick moment of shock as he went down with her, down with her white arms round him, into the darkness. He gave no cry when he fell. The night was still, until a chill little wind like the steps of the dead shivered its way across the moor, sighing down the hillside to where the small farm lay hushed and empty in its hollow.

Presently, down the road the woman returned, her gaunt figure dark and unlovely in the spreading moonlight. Down the path thudded the tramp of her boots. She opened the door, and seeing he was not there, a shiver

of apprehension went through her. 'Father'—
she called shrilly. 'Dad—where are you—?'

She went to the foot of the stairs, to his
room, and to her husband, still busy about the
sheds in the yard.

'He's gone,' she said. 'The old man's gone.'

'Gone? What do you mean?'

She did not answer. One look at her face was
enough.

They searched for hours. But it was not until
the morning he was found ... lying stiff and
frozen at the bottom of the shaft ... gnarled
fingers clenched with ice, as though enclosing
something infinitely precious, beneath a drift
of newly fallen snow.

CHAPTER TEN

THE UNKNOWN SHORE

The last thing I remembered was flouncing out of my Fleet Street office sick of the whole human 'rat-race', until I found myself in the train with Cordelia bound for Cornwall. The rest was a blank; except of course Cordelia's wild suggestion in her father's garden of our mad elopement. All the rest was hazy, a jig-saw affair composed of bits and pieces vaguely realised, then falling out of place again so nothing made sense.

I simply couldn't understand it; but although puzzled, one fact was clear above my mental aberration ... I was at last doing what I wanted to.

Cordelia was looking particularly dishy. But then she was that kind of girl, slim and delicately proportioned, with a pale pointed face wide at the cheek bones, and quite fabulous black lashed grey eyes that had a vague, smoky look. She was wearing a sort of greeny-blue suit that day, with a violet cape thing slung over her shoulders. Her hair, the sort of silky fawn kind you can't pin down to any exact shade, turned in just below her ears, like a page-boy's, and although she didn't look exactly trendy, she was certainly with it. She always would be whatever she wore. Dressed carelessly in a shirt and jeans, or the most expensive model gown, either slinky silk or voluminous frail 'see-through', Cordelia could throw anything on and look like a million dollars. Her accessories were frequently off-beat to put it politely, or forgotten altogether. It just didn't matter. Her vagueness to detail was part of her charm. Anyway I was besotted by her and to find that I'd actually allowed myself to be manipulated into this mad project, didn't really surprise me, although I knew there'd be a reckoning with her father sometime. Still, there I was, a struggling sub-editor with hardly a bean in the bank, setting off on the adventure of a lifetime with the heiress only daughter of millionaire Carew-Scott.

Trying to think back I made an effort to pin-point our first meeting; but the memory wouldn't click. It must have been at some social function or sporting event. I *did* recall dimly though that the old man hadn't approved, and that following a crisis our relationship had become a secret affair ... something precariously balanced on the edge always of exposure and collapse.

Of course Cordelia, being Cordelia, wasn't the type to forego anything she really wanted; so here we were, bound for the wilds of Cornwall where apparently she'd purchased the 'loveliest, most divine' cottage in the world.

162

I should have been enraptured, and I was. But I wished I could remember.

There was an unreal quality about the whole thing that at odd moments took a little of the magic away. Not Cordelia's magic ... this by then was an integral part of me. But the prospect of a life ahead with *any* woman, even the most adorable creature in the world, had its limitations when memory was lacking. There were things we couldn't share; moments of decision, of taking the 'leap' together, of looking back and saying, 'do you remember how we had to sneak out ...?' or 'the day before was sheer hell. There was I, doing...', perhaps 'I thought someone must guess...' oh any number of intimate personal understandings that lovers reminisce over later and giggle about, once togetherness is safely achieved.

I couldn't do that. The only clue to the past I had was by subtly probing Cordelia's mind, and making a pattern for myself. I didn't even know whether we were married or not, but I supposed we were, because she had a wedding ring on the third finger of the left hand. This didn't prove anything of course. It could be for appearances' sake. And if not that ... but it was inconceivable she could have married anyone else. The odd thing was she didn't refer to any ceremony at all, just sat in the carriage looking dreamy and luscious and so expensively secure I dare hardly touch her.

'Shy, David?' She queried once, snuggling up to me with her cheek lightly resting against my shoulder, close to my own. I could feel a silky tendril of hair brushing my face, catch the frail drift of perfume that temporarily swept me from reality into a world of enchantment peculiarly Cordelia's, a world of excitement and heady anticipation; of eternal springtime. 'Oh, Cordelia,' I murmured with my lips suddenly warm and gentle on her own. 'Cordelia ... Cordelia ...'

It was like that, on and off, for most of that long journey; an awareness of ecstatic fulfilment to come, alternating with practical interludes in the dining carriage of eating, and drinking just sufficient, but not too much, then back again to our first class compartment, where we sat in a daze of mutual adoration interspersed with perfunctory glances at newspapers and magazines.

From undulating country of green fields and pleasant villages huddled picturesquely into folds of gentle hills, the vista became gradually more open and windswept. Once over the river Tamar, blissful content became charged gradually with a mounting sense of exhilaration, of that Cornish magic and mystery which can be found nowhere else in the world.

Yet with it, also, I felt awe, a certain queer feeling of disbelief that even the cool touch of Cordelia's hand over my own couldn't dispel.

164

'What's the matter?' she said once. 'Why are you so quiet?'

'Fear maybe,' I answered, almost involuntarily.

'Fear?' Her voice was incredulous.

I couldn't bear the brief pain in her eyes; all I wanted was to give reassurance. But in a burst of honesty the truth was torn from me.

'Cordelia ... I don't know how to say this but I must, before you go into something you don't know about. The fact is I'm not quite what you think. I'm ...'

A burst of soft laughter subdued the sound of the train's steady rhythm before she said, still with an underlying giggle in her voice, 'Oh dear! I'm shattered. You mean I'm rushing headlong into the future with a dark horse, one of those dreadful men having a host of affairs tucked away in a very shady past ...?' She sobered, controlled her mirth for a moment, before adding, '*Is* that what you mean, darling? And do you suppose for one moment it would ...'

'Cordelia,' I interrupted, 'you must listen. No, it's not that. Nothing like it. I only wish it was.'

'Then what?'

'I've lost my memory.'

'Your *memory*? Well ...' She considered a moment before asking me quietly, 'Is that so important after all?'

'Of *course* it's important,' I said. 'To both of

us. Especially you. I can't even remember how I got into the train. Only rushing from some bloody office because I was so browned off with the whole...'

'What?' Her voice was a whisper.

'Set-up I suppose,' I told her. 'The next I knew was to find myself sitting by you in this select compartment bound for Cornwall and your dream cottage. But apart from that ... except for very far-off things of course, including your father's natural animosity, I just haven't a clue. Oh I *do* recall falling in love with you, that's one thing that hasn't changed...'

'And isn't it the most important?'

'Yes. Of course. But the fact remains that somewhere in the background I *must* have commitments, people I know ... relationships; well, mustn't I?' I asked rather feebly.

She didn't answer for a moment, then she said, 'I suppose we all have, darling, all of us born into this funny old world. We don't just grow like Topsy. There are bound to be people pushing in and muddling us up, and that's why so many make a hash of things. I mean, what matters is to find the *one good* thing. Isn't it?'

When she looked at me in that certain way with her eyes all luminous and brimming, I knew I hadn't a chance.

'Cordelia,' I murmured, kissing her lips gently. 'Of course. But sometime soon, you must tell me about myself. Will you do that? So

166

that the whole of me can be with you, the past, the now, and the future. Will you do that?'

She nodded. 'If I have to. But I don't think I will. You won't mind ... in the end.'

As I relaxed later, I realised I hadn't asked her even if we were married, probably the most important thing of all. Possibly without realising it, I'd shied from it. According to current society, marriage wasn't an essential of a shared happy life, and I didn't want to appear too conventionally hide-bound in her eyes. Being with her should be enough. And it was; it surely was. But what of tomorrow? And yesterday? ... The years lost that should be mine, as a whole man, to present to her simply because she was so precious to me? The past could be hurtful perhaps, but in surrendering it I would at least be proving my fidelity ... showing her I was prepared to give something up. With things as they were, there was nothing.

Except Cordelia herself.

The late afternoon gradually turned to evening, with the first star hanging in a greenish sky over the darkening land. Against the horizon the far glitter of sea quivered intermittently in splashed white against rising lumps of rock. I fancied the tang of brine and heather in the drift of air from the window, watching at the same time, a silvered swoop of seagulls from a stone-walled field. Instinctively my hand sought Cordelia's again, and pressed it so that momentarily the delicate bones seemed to contract and disintegrate. Then, from their gentle rhythmic pulse, I knew she was real and living, beside me, a part of that wonderful dream-in-life so rarely apprehended or experienced.

There was a deep yet communicable silence between us in which part of her seemed to become myself, and my own body and spirit infused with hers. Time mattered no more. Our oneness was that of things beyond mortal comprehension, and I knew that however intricate the pattern that had brought me to her, it was inevitable. A rounding-off of some compulsive dream, having its course only through her.

When we reached Penzance it was almost dark. We took a taxi to Penagwallow, and by then the whole landscape was muted into a fantastic pattern of blues, greys, and silvered lemon from a rising moon. The lane winding steeply towards the coast twisted pale and ribbon-like between high wind-blown hedges until the undergrowth cleared abruptly showing the rim of headland outlined dark against the glittering water. Ahead, on the right, a mellow light streamed from a window and open door of a humped low building.

'That's it,' Cordelia whispered, with repressed excitement in her voice. 'That's the cottage. When I saw it I knew it was right, the only one for us ... just you and me, darling.

And Mrs Peters, of course, in the daytime. She comes from a farm. I told her to be waiting...' her voice died on a note of anxiety. 'Oh David ... don't you *like* it?'

I laughed quietly. 'My dear love, I haven't seen it yet. But ... it's rather remote, isn't it?'

'That's what you wanted; you *said* so ... you *always* said so.' She sounded suddenly panic-stricken, like a child, and for some reason I felt so too. But I tried to reassure her.

'It's wonderful. Just what I've dreamed of always.' And this was true. Why was it then that when brought face to face with the reality of the dream I felt suddenly a faint tug of apprehension and doubt.

I squeezed her hand hard, and a moment later the car stopped. The driver was a silent man saying nothing but the price of the fare which I handed to him with a generous tip.

When the thrum of the engine had died round a bend of the lane, Cordelia, still with her hand in mine, turned her face up to me; such a fragile, flower-like face, petal pale in the frail moonlight. I kissed her, drawing the sweetness of her being into mine, realising in a stab of wonder how crude my former assessment of her had been—'dishy', ... a 'gorgeous girl'—Cordelia was more than that; far far more. And the knowledge curiously disturbed me. Though close in spirit ... closer than I'd ever imagined two human beings could be, I felt at the same time alone with a

169

tremendous responsibility before me. All of her was mine now, for the taking, the perfect image of my physical and heart's desire. But ... what was the 'but' so troubling me? And why were we two standing like beings of another world, hand in hand, on the fringe it seemed, of time itself, staring under the stars across that vista of land and sea? There was no sound, no rustle of earth or air, only the solitary night, and the deepening reddish glow of the light streaming from the cottage.

Cordelia urged me forward gently. Her slim hand was cold in mine. 'Come, darling,' she whispered. 'Once we're inside it will be all right; honestly, I promise.'

I couldn't move for a moment; I didn't doubt her, but the knowledge, the sudden implication of what decision could mean—renouncement of any past I'd had, any secret commitments of my buried life—held me rooted at the gates of this small place she'd planned as our sanctuary. I think something like a repressed sob, such as that of an animal in pain, forced me against my will to take a few steps ahead. The interior of the cottage glowed warm and inviting, though a thin blue haze of mist quivered about the door.

'Well?' Cordelia whispered against my ear.

I was suddenly frantic with fear.

'Cordelia ... darling ... I can't. I won't. Try to understand...'

I lurched back. She turned. The warm glow

spluttered and faded, becoming one with the washed pale light of the moon and stars, catching her face with an eerie bluish clarity, dimming her lovely eyes to enormous dark pools of shadows, and her hair to cloud.

And as I stared, the youthful face began to sag and age into a face no longer hers but dimly recorded in my mind. I tried to call her name. Whether she heard or not I didn't know, but over a rising moaning of thin wind through the undergrowth I caught the sad-sweet echo of her voice.

'Just a dream, darling. A dream of youth. Go back to your world, the one you know. You don't need me ... you never have ... away ... away ...'

From somewhere nearby a gull rose screaming into the night sky. Automatically I looked round. There was no cottage, no welcoming light, only the stark clear edge of the gaunt cliffs leading to the point of no return. I dragged myself round, trying to force my legs to movement.

Then, suddenly the sky lowered in an immense curtain of darkness, and I knew nothing any more.

*   *   *

Very slowly consciousness returned. Above me light quivered, died, faded, then returned again in a haze of shivering lines like those of the

171

early morning sun lifting over a cold spring sea. I was lying flat and thought I must have fallen on to the sand. But there was no sand beneath me, only comforting warmth filling me with an indescribable sense of security and peace. Memory gradually registered, and I looked round for Cordelia. She was not there of course, and though it shouldn't have the knowledge meant tremendous relief, because I knew our journey into the might-have-been had no substance in the real life I had already built for myself. Why then had I travelled so far? And for what? A journey of the mind only from one point to another like the inevitable rising and ebbing of the tide on an empty shore? But then no shore was ever empty; each breaking of a single wave brought a disturbance of sand; a throwing up of minute particles of natural material to make an ever-changing pattern for exploration.

Sea ... sand ... designs man-made and of nature. Darkness, and then light. Yes; light. Suddenly it hit me, a blaze of realisation as a woman's face took radiance from the curdling air and came down to me. Feminine, yet tired, and not young any more. A face that, like my job, had begun at times to bore me utterly, reminding me how inevitably youth had passed, sending me eventually on a last wild bid for the years long gone.

Eve. My wife.

How sad she looked, yet hopeful, a little

tremulous as her lips brushed my forehead, and she asked, 'How're you feeling David? Is it too bad?'

Life was slowly beginning to register, in little pulses of darting pain; legs, back, head, even in my toes, which I found with a certain grim satisfaction I could still wiggle.

'What happened?' I asked in a voice that hardly seemed to register.

'You had an accident,' she said, 'crossing the road from the office. A car got you.'

Of course.

The truth hit me like a bomb.

'How long ... and where ...?'

'You're in hospital,' she said gently, 'But the doctors say you should be all right. Oh David, if you hadn't been ...'

Slowly the tears gathered and fell from her eyes ... those eyes that had once enchanted me as much as Cordelia's, although differently. Naturally there was a difference. There had to be. Real life was no fairy-tale, no leap into the unseen with an impossible love. Really quite an ordinary affair, yet extraordinary in its tenacity to survive and when the occasion came, to fight back.

For a pause of time that could have been an eternity, but in reality must have been only seconds, I recalled my struggle on the edge of the abyss, my refusal, even with Cordelia's help, to take that last step into mortal disintegration. Yes, it would have been mortal.

Because Cordelia was dead. She had died twenty years ago in a boating accident, shortly following our final break up. Even then, when I was a young man, I had shied at any ultimate commitment to her.

Why?

Possibly because I hadn't loved enough. To be *in* love was one thing. Loving quite another.

And I loved Eve.

For the first time, a moment before the nurse came in, I saw her clearly as she really was ... middle-aged, with the first bloom gone, and the small weary lines of experience etched about her eyes and mouth. But beautiful in a way I'd chosen to disregard for far too long.

I tried to tell her so; but how can a man explain something in him he doesn't even understand himself? There was no point in saying, 'In future I'll stick to my job and not grumble, and never lose patience or wish to hell we were back where we started. I'll never close my eyes tight wishing for the impossible dream. What's good is here and real ... with you and our two kids...' no; one didn't say such things, because promises made in the throes of reaction had a knack of turning sour at future moments, and of course we'd have these moments; everyone did. They were a part of existence.

So I stopped mumbling, and suddenly she smiled. Well ... it was almost a laugh ... a funny sort of musical sound in her throat.

'You old silly,' she said. 'Stop it. I'll put up with your ghosts and dreams just so long as I have the real you. And that's honest, David.'

She bent down to me and touched my lips with her own.

And when I closed my eyes she was neither Eve nor Cordelia, but both of them merged into one; and we were walking along a pale shore with only the gulls flying overhead and the morning beckoning from the rim of the waking world.

CHAPTER ELEVEN

WAIT TILL THE SPRING

Three months after the riding accident which meant that Laura Winter would never walk again, her parents, who were devoted to her, sold their expensive house in the city suburbs and moved to forest country bordering the Welsh Marches where they had spent many happy holidays.

Laura who was just twenty expressed neither pleasure nor the reverse at the change. Indeed her attitude to life in general appeared completely detached and uninterested. She didn't complain; if she had it would have seemed more natural. Instead she accepted those first days in a wheel-chair without demur, adapting herself automatically to its mechanical contraptions, learning by its aid and other devious means to do much for herself that until then had been impossible. But she never smiled. It was as though the lovely vital girl she'd once been had changed into another hardly recognisable to her family. Her good looks remained, but on a frailer scale ... red gold hair, framing a pale heart shaped face that before had been rich with the bloom of youth; hazel eyes flecked with green, solemn now, and somehow condemning, giving her a curious withdrawn look that frequently made her parents uncomfortable.

All that first autumn and winter she spoke very little, spending her time mostly in her bedroom thumbing the pages of a book idly, or staring out of the window. The view from there was quiet and dreamlike, spreading from lush fields to the mysterious shadowed forest with its constantly changing shades of deep green merging into misty blues, and darkest purple flecked with orange and gold. Yet she expressed no wish to go there, although a special invalid self-driven vehicle had been ordered for her, in which, she was told, she would soon be able to steer for herself and explore the paths for a short way.

The forest, which was directly adjoining her home was conservation property, held by the National Trust. Much of it had been re-planted with pines already reaching tall and feathery towards the sky. The paths there were wide and carefully kept, smelling tangy and sweet from resinous growth. But smaller tracks wound more haphazardly into wilder and more natural terrain, where ancient oaks, spreading beeches, and sloes entangled with thorn, mingled together in huddled thickets interspersed with sudden pale green clearings.

'There are a lot of birds there, Laura,' Adele Winter told her daughter. 'Do you remember how you used to love bird-watching when you were a child ...?'

178

'Yes.'

'When you feel like it, when the spring comes, you'll be able to go there ... not too far of course, but think how nice it will be on a fine day, to go out by yourself if you like, and even take your sketching things. Or your recorder perhaps? The bird song I'm sure is...'

'Oh, stop it, stop it,' Laura cried suddenly with a shrill sharp note in her voice. 'Who cares!'

Her mother, rebuffed, turned away, trying not to show the tears in her eyes.

'It's no use,' she told her husband. 'Laura's changed completely. She *shouted* at me just now. It's as if...' she hesitated before continuing, '... do you think there's anything else, John, some brain-damage that's altered her personality?'

'They'd have said so if there was,' John Winter answered quietly. 'It's a matter of coming to terms, I'm afraid, and it can't be easy for a girl like Laura, just starting life and so full of vitality and joy...'

'Not any more,' his wife interrupted dully. 'She's no initiative left and certainly no joy. After all how can you expect it?'

'We must hope,' he said stubbornly. 'Wait till the spring comes. Everything takes up with the spring.'

'Does it?' Adele's tones were bitter. 'I wonder.'

John's prophecy to a certain extent proved

179

to be true. When the first celandines opened in the hedgerows followed by clumps of primroses and violets, Laura for the first time ventured outside alone. The forest was pale feathery green then, lit by frail sunshine to gold. When rain fell, it was softly, bringing new young growth overnight that left a radiance everywhere. Even Laura's deadness stirred into slow awareness of awakening life.

First she merely propelled herself to the edge of the lawn bordering the woods, where she sat staring into the whispering world of shadowed mystery and intangible half-sensed magic. Then the next day, which was fine, she went through the garden gates along the main forest path for a short way, drawing the deep sweet smell of pines and herbage into her lungs, listening to the hundred mingled small sounds of stirring branches and bird song ... of drifting grass and secret small calls of insects and hidden wild creatures from the wood's dark heart.

With her eyes intent on the persistent movement of lurking shadows, and transient patterned sunlight dappling the ground, a deep longing, though unavowed, rose in her to explore the narrower paths threading ribbon-like through the thickening trees and undergrowth.

Something unseen, yet vibrant with life and meaning beckoned her insidiously into the untrodden wilderness; an urge to become one with the singing sighing sounds of wind through the spreading arms of oak and ash and clustered hazel, to ride like some legendary queen beneath the immense cathedral shapes of lofty beech, away from the world she'd once known into a deeper sphere of understanding where no pitying human words or half averted glances could intrude.

Dignity.

Yes, for the first time since her accident, a sense of independence and pride filled her. Here perhaps, she could learn to face her future with equanimity, knowing that a secret world waited to receive her.

When she got back to the house later, her parents couldn't fail to notice the difference, though they'd learned by then not to comment on her moods of rebellion and long silences.

'What was it like in the wood, Laura?' Adele asked in assumed practical tones. 'Pleasant? Or a bit chilly. You mustn't...' she stopped herself before Laura could react in her habitual tart way, reserved for people who fussed.

'It was all right,' Laura answered non-committally. 'Quite nice actually. I shall take my sketching with me one day, and perhaps my recorder. There are lots of birds there.'

'What a good idea,' her father said. 'A bit of painting, eh?' He laughed superficially. 'Wish I was a dab hand with the brush like you. Wouldn't surprise me if you were famous one day.'

If only he *wouldn't*; Laura thought with the old familiar nagging despair rising up in her. Fame? Success? Such meaningless words when they belonged to a world she'd never know any more, to the world of mobile bodies ... sport, laughter, dancing and parties. Riding over the hills on her beloved mare Starlight; all the joyous natural things she'd been born to. Ambition was a dead thing without the opportunity for enjoying the results of it.

In any case she'd never wanted to make a name for herself. Until the accident her hopes had been merely those of any other normal attractive girl; to have a full life in some sphere or other until she met someone ... the right man, so they could settle down together, make a home, and have children. Now, that would never happen; and it was no use pretending. She didn't to herself, so why must others? Why couldn't someone just for once, say to her, 'Right. You're an invalid for life. So get on with it and for God's sake don't grumble. Others have gone through worse than you, so don't expect sympathy, it won't do a thing for you.'

She knew all that, and at last had come to accept it. But she couldn't tolerate pretence or pity, which was the reason for her silences and withdrawal from human affection.

During the days that followed she spent increasingly more time navigating the winding paths of the forest. No one realised how far she

182

went, or perhaps there'd have been objections and restraint imposed in some subtle way on her movements. Occasionally she took paintings of birds and flowers back to the house, delicate water colours with a subtle sense of light about them, skilfully blended into designs suggesting more than was actually there.

'They really are quite delightful,' a friend of John's, an art dealer, said one day, after viewing the collection. 'Extremely original too. When you have a few more, Laura, it's possible I could arrange an exhibition in a small London gallery I know.'

'Thank you,' Laura said in a cool remote voice. 'It's very kind of you.'

But she was not really interested. Her pleasure had been in depicting what she'd felt and seen. The thought of having her work viewed and criticised was actually rather obnoxious to her, though of course no one would have understood why.

April passed into May and June, with long golden days broken only by occasional rain.

One late afternoon when the sun was lowering in the western sky, Laura set off unknown to anyone for the forest, determined this time to penetrate deeper darker territory. Usually she rested at that hour, which was why Adele and John had taken the chance to slip off in the car to the nearest small town for shopping.

The housekeeper had her afternoon out, and the girl, who'd already cleared away tea, was too immersed in a new magazine, *Glamour*, to catch the soft whirring sounds of the invalid vehicle passing down the hall and out through the open door.

Only a slight breeze stirred the trees as Laura entered the forest, gently shivering through the feathered pines and firs, casting beckoning velvet shadows from the thickening woodland.

A hundred yards or so along the main track she cut off to her left, steering down a narrow path bordered by larch, ferns, twisting sloes and thorn which eventually merged into the land's natural habitat of oak and beech. Through intertwined branches the sunlight filtered in transient gold. Birds chirruped lazily as she passed, a small wild creature darted from the undergrowth under a scurry of leaves. Otherwise loneliness and quietness reigned. When she reached the dome of ancient beeches she paused for a moment or two listening to the silence of nature that was not really silent at all, but filled with the pulsing thrusting murmur of growing things. Then she went on, not sure of what called her, or how far her destination might be. On an impulse of identification with that untrammelled world, she tore her hair from its band and let the bright fair glow of her hair fall in a silky sea over her shoulders, rippled to music by the frail breeze.

At last she came to a clearing of palest grass,

a circle almost, surrounded by tall and gracious elms and beech linked with sturdy oaks. Peace, in a spreading tide of wonder filled her, flooding her body with warmth so her numbed dead limbs pricked and pulsed in communication. She lifted her arms to the domed green and russet ceiling, palms outstretched and lapped to gold from the fitful light. Then her hands strayed to the neck of her dress and loosened it, with the cream virgin skin radiant and glorified by her own beauty.

Then as she lifted her eyes to a blue patch of sky between the tracery of branches, she heard it. Faintly at first, then gathering momentum with every second that passed. The rhythmic rise and fall of a man's voice singing with such anguish of fulfilment and loss that the whole forest, from its subdued murmur, became completely still and hushed into reverence and awe of its own.

Laura's hands tightened on the arms of her car. Her spirit swelled and expanded, as the deep throbbing melody echoed and thrilled from tree to tree, taking the whole terrain into one tremendous glorification of creation.

And it seemed then the secret of all things was hers ... of pain and joy ... of waking mornings and flying clouds ... of birth and defeat; of striving and dying; the ultimate meaning of life caught up into the vast symphony of universal being.

Time ceased while she listened and stared.

Stared until the fading sunlight was resolved before her eyes into a shivering golden ball of fire, encompassing all the world by one final burst of flame.

Then it disintegrated as the last note finally died leaving only a column of cloud before her, licked to a pale quivering glow at its trembling edges.

Laura still sat speechless and without movement, watching the shape gradually materialise into that of a male figure standing quiet and ebony dark against the muted shadows of the trees.

He had his hands outstretched towards her, like those of some ancient atavistic god, yet infinitely tender, calling upon her to give that in herself which for so long had been dormant around her.

In the morning they found her, with her chair still erect a few feet away. How she'd moved from it at all no one ever knew; but in her face was such a look of serenity and wonder that none could grieve for her ... only marvel at death's compensation for a wounded life.

*   *   *

It was not until after the funeral that Laura's parents learned another, perhaps significant, factor about the spot where she'd died.

'It's odd,' the local doctor told them over drinks one night, 'that she should have fallen

186

just there.'

'What do you mean?' Adele asked.

'Oh ... some ten years or so ago there was another tragedy,' their new friend remarked reminiscently. 'A young coloured man, a singer with a more than promising career before him collapsed at the identical place. Of course he'd brought it on himself ... in a way. He'd been ill you see ... heart, and had been told he must never on *any account* project his voice again with any force. In fact the verdict was, his career was finished.'

'Hm! sad.' John murmured.

'Yes. I knew him quite well, as a matter of fact, a fine chap, lots of courage too. He came to the district to recuperate and rest and appeared to accept the decision. But it's my belief he never did. And though the cause of death was undoubtedly a coronary ... I'm sure he welcomed and went to meet it. In my opinion...' there was a short pause before he continued ... 'the frustrated joy of living became too much for him and he just went there to sing his heart out. It's a lovely spot you know ... reverberant somehow with nature and...' he hesitated, '... unsullied things. I've been there myself occasionally at twilight and listened to the silence. Maybe a hardened old medico like me shouldn't resort to such rhapsody ... but it seems to me only one way properly describes it ... a silence holding all the music of the gods ... if you know what I mean.'

187

They didn't; how could they? For very few have the luck or perception to catch even an echo of that unknown chord torn from the earth's deep womb. The receptacle for the greatest mystery of all to be woken each spring by the secret whisper of life eternal ... and a singing ... singing ... which goes on and on, forever.

CHAPTER TWELVE

THE BELL

The mist was thickening every moment. I had an injured limb, and we were lost.

'We can't stay here,' Vernon said, maddeningly quoting the obvious, 'the only thing's to get you down somewhere; that ankle could be broken.'

'I'm pretty damn sure it is,' I told him, as agonising stabs of pain shot from my swollen foot in the knee. 'But get down? *How?* Short of a miracle it seem we're stuck here till the morning *if* we survive at all, which seems doubtful.'

Vernon got up, swinging his arms over his chest, as the grey air billowed and curdled round, creeping through our windcheaters and every chink of clothing, sucking the warmth from our limbs while I wondered why we'd not turned back earlier when the first sign of grey appeared above the valley of Tywarth. But the weather prospect for that week-end had been good, and my friend Vernon and I, on vacation from teaching, had thought a bit of rambling and mountain climbing would be a welcome change, after months of tutoring obtuse college boys.

That particular morning had been still and

clear with no sign of impending wind or cloud. We'd eaten our sandwiches half way up Hellescarne, then started off again up the rock-strewn slope towards the summit, skirting the precipitous Devil's Gap on one side, and on the other the dangerous 'Three Maidens' where a step out of place could mean a fall to certain death. The route planned was one for walkers rather than experienced climbers, which professionally we were not, and the prospect had seemed to us child's play. Both of us had climbed most of the gentler peaks of Britain, and Hellescarne tipping three thousand feet or so, was simple enough, tackled from the right angle.

We hadn't a moment's anxiety until the mist came up, and then to my dismay and disgust at my own carelessness I'd slipped down a shale slide, landing with my foot buckled under me at right angles.

When I'd extricated myself I couldn't move for pain until Vernon clambered down to the rescue.

Luckily we'd brandy with us, a bit of chocolate and two sandwiches left over from mid-day. Both of us took a swig of the spirit and then settled down ... if 'settle' can be used to describe such physical agony ... to review the situation.

The mist by then had thickened into a cloak. I couldn't walk on my own, and except for a small torch and compass we hadn't a thing to

190

help us. We must still have been about three thousand feet up, with the Gap and the Maidens waiting greedily below if we took the wrong direction. Yet a night in the damp and cold could be dangerous, and except for pain I didn't know I had a right leg any more.

'We'll have to take a chance,' Vernon said suddenly, switching on his torch to get as clear a view as possible of the compass. 'If we strike directly west we should be able to make it.' He paused before adding, 'If *you* can. I've got a pretty hefty arm. Also...' forcing a laugh, 'there's still enough of "what killed Aunty" in the flask to give us a reasonable send off.'

He waited: and sensing the anxiety underlying his forced banter, I replied more optimistically than I felt, 'O.K. Let's get going.'

I was steeling myself for the effort when something startled us to brief immobility—the drawn-out eerie tolling of a distant bell somewhere below.

'Good heavens!' Vernon exclaimed. 'Who'd have thought it? A bell; must be from a church somewhere. But I didn't know... there wasn't a hamlet marked on the map, not to the north-west, was there, Andy?'

I shook my head. To tell the truth I was feeling so sick and paralytic with pain by then I couldn't have cared what was or wasn't marked on the map. All I wanted was to be away from that infernal mountain into

191

civilisation again.

'I don't know,' I said, 'you're the guide.'

'Well, if we keep good track of direction the bell should be a bit of help as well. Come on, man, hang on to my arm like hell and grit your teeth. Sorry I can't do more, but maybe the good spirits are out on our side for once.'

I don't know why, but his particular allusion to the unseen at that moment jarred and depressed rather than cheered me. It was like being in some macabre weird other-world, encompassed as we were by the cloying clouds of vapour with only the mournful tolling of the bell indicating life below.

But what life?

As we progressed slowly, with difficulty, stopping every few yards or so to examine the compass, I was filled with a queer and mounting foreboding, expecting every moment to take a step into some yawning chasm waiting with hungry elemental consciousness for human prey.

I had never felt this way on any mountain before. Possibly my physical condition had heightened my imaginative senses, or lessened any lingering consciousness of reality I possessed. All I was aware of as I hobbled ... or rather hopped along with one arm clutching Vernon's mercilessly ... was an increasing sense of approaching doom, of fear so indescribable I stopped at one point and said, 'Look Vernon. I'm all in. You go on. I'll wait here. And then if you can get help I'll survive. Heavens, man, I'm not sick. I've only snapped a bone, and the quicker you get down there the better.'

But he refused.

'There can't be more than a thousand feet now. And the going's easier. We've missed the Gap, and the Maidens are far behind. The mist's getting no worse...'

'How could it?' I snapped. 'Nothing could be worse than this.'

But presently I went on with him, following the pale furred circle thrown by the torch at our feet, negotiating with difficulty each tump of earth and rock, pausing at moments to rest, then starting off again. Sweat mingling with the damned fog poured in rivulets down my forehead, though my body alternately burned with fire then cooled as abruptly to icy chill. Then, to make matters worse, the torch went out.

Vernon muttered something under his breath not fit for human ears, seated himself on a tump of earth, with his head in his hands, getting to his feet again just as quickly.

'Come on.' He shook me by the shoulder. 'We're not stopping now. There's heather here. That means we've passed the worst of it. And the bell. Can you hear it? Nearer. Much nearer.'

Oh yes I heard it.

Long, drawn-out, incredibly mournful and terrifying.

'I don't like it,' I said. 'It's not ... it's not ...'

'What?'

'Right somehow.'

'What do you mean right? It's the most welcome sound I've heard in a month of Sundays. Pull yourself together, man. Stick it ... *please*, Andy old chap. I know it's hell for you but I reckon we're nearer than we thought. Look ...'

I wiped the moisture from my eyes and stared ahead. It seemed to me the fog was lifting slightly. And after a minute or two a bank of it rolled away leaving the slope furred but visible; an incline of turf and furze interspersed with tumbled boulders above a shrouded valley of indefinite looming shapes.

And still the bell tolled. I pulled back automatically. Vernon turned his head.

'What's the matter? Only a couple of hundred yards or so.'

'I don't like it.' I said, repeating my former opinion, 'It's ... wrong somehow.'

'For heaven's sake ...' he broke off impatiently.

'It's not Sunday, it's not the time for any bell to go on and on like that. Vernon, if you insist on getting down to that place I'm staying here. Then, when you've found out whether you can get help or not, which I doubt, you can come for me.'

'Oh! very well. But a bit further. For *Pete's*

sake!...' his voice was on edge. I knew he was rattled; so I gave in and went on with him until we reached a small flat plateau of rock hedged in by heather, where I could sit in a reasonably unimpeded position with my leg out, and see what went on below. The fog was clearing quickly by then, and as Vernon made his way down, the bell abruptly stopped tolling. A sudden pale beam of light like that of the dying sun or rising moon—I had lost count of time—lit the scene to strange clarity, showing a square tower rising from an ivory-white rectangular building. But there was no hamlet; no cottage or house visible; just that erection of pale granite or possibly marble, with a few tall shining stones placed at intervals around.

When Vernon's figure reached the base of the mountain I saw him pause for a moment before moving ahead again.

And then, from the grouped shadows to my left, a moving column of dark clad beings gradually emerged, winding in single file towards the building. They were mostly small, and slim, reaching only slightly above Vernon's waist, but emitting a curious hypnotic power that held my eyes riveted to the spectacle. In contrast to the black clothes, their complexions were alabaster pale, their hair white; some old with long beards, others with shining white hair falling around youthful ivory-white faces to their shoulders. The males carried swords shaped as scythes; the women who followed behind, had their hands pressed together above their breasts as though in supplication.

Written down now the scene appears to hold no particular terror. But to me the effect was one of dread and inexplicable horror ... especially when Vernon stepped forward, one hand up as though in salutation.

The leader stopped, lifted an arm in reply, then with his free hand, touched my friend on his forehead. Vernon moved back, and the procession continued; a sombre crocodile of swathed black shapes turning into the building. Gradually the vista changed, and as the square gap of the door closed upon the last figure, all was taken into mist again. There was no shining building, no sign left of the white skinned white-haired throng; only the dim silhouette of what could have been a great rock or rising hillside, and Vernon scrambling from there towards the base of the mountain.

'There's a chapel there all right,' he said when he reached me, 'and I was lucky. A service about to start ... that's what the bell was. I was asked to join, and would have if it hadn't been for you. Still, maybe I'll go back one day.'

It seemed to me he was over-excited. His voice had a higher note about it than usual.

'A *chapel*?' I echoed.

'Yes,' he agreed more quietly.

'Well it looked pretty odd from here. I didn't

like what I could see of that crowd.'

'A perfectly ordinary congregation,' he said, hardly convincingly. 'And most helpful. The Minister ... or whatever you like to call him ... gave me a clear guide to our whereabouts. We have to cut slightly to the right, take the gradual slope down and we should be on the road to Llanherrick in no time. So if you feel like making the effort we'd better get going.'

I didn't feel like any effort just then; my leg was hurting like hell, and my head was throbbing. But anything was better than spending another minute near that awful fog-bound place; so with Vernon's help I got to my feet, or rather one foot, and started off.

The journey back to the inn was a painful, silent, affair. To get my mind away from my own plight, I flung out one or two probing questions concerning Vernon's brief contact with the strange white-haired leader of the weird throng. But following his first excitement he'd relapsed into a curiously withdrawn mood, speaking only occasionally in monosyllables, with obvious reluctance to share the experience. I was in such a state of exhaustion when we reached Llanherrick that I began to doubt what had seemed at the time to be the factual evidence of my own eyes.

And then in the lamplight of the hall, I saw the mark. A curious triangular red scar in the middle of my friend's forehead. Small, but very distinctive, as though etched into the skin

197

finely by a very thin pen or nail.

'What's that?' I asked abruptly.

'What?'

'You've got a mark on your forehead, Vernon. Just there...' indicating the position on my own brow.

'Oh.' He laughed self-consciously, as his hand strayed upwards. 'It's nothing. A bramble or something, I guess.'

There was a short pause before he demanded querulously, 'What the devil are you getting at? What's a scratch, for Pete's sake? You should be worrying about yourself and how we're going to get a doctor in this godforsaken place.'

He turned away, but not quickly enough to hide the sudden slightly shifty half-frightened look in his eyes.

I was puzzled. More than that, concerned, and if I'd thought I had a chance of getting one more word out of him I'd have persisted in questioning. But I knew there was none, and naturally in the hubbub of getting medical aid and arrangements for X-rays of my leg and ankle, the subject was pushed aside.

I had a compound fracture which meant my holiday was cut short by a spell of hospitalisation. I saw Vernon only once for a few minutes before the vacation ended, as he had to spend a period in town preceding the autumn session. Whilst he was with me he did not seem disposed to discuss the Llanherrick episode; but I noticed the mark still glowed bright on his forehead, and knew his explanation of being scratched by a bramble as mere fabrication.

As it happened we were not to meet again for three years. That winter I heard he'd taken a lecturing post abroad somewhere, which meant our paths didn't cross before he went. He sent a card to me from out East, to which I replied eventually, briefly and with the minimum of news, being a notoriously bad correspondent. After that there was a complete silence between us until we ran into each other quite by chance at a London club in the late summer of 1976.

He was looking extremely fit, bronzed and lean, and appeared glad to see me.

'Andy, old man,' he said, 'what a surprise. I was going to look you up of course. But I only got back to the old country a week ago—and that sounds like a good old fashioned colonial speaking, I guess!'

I laughed. 'No matter. What are...' I stopped suddenly, as the light caught his forehead, and was about to continue when he forestalled me.

'Oh, the mark. Yes, still there.' He tossed off his drink. 'Doesn't worry me. In fact I'm rather proud of it. Quite distinguished looking, don't you think?'

I didn't reply. The thing seemed damned odd to me, and the truth was I felt mildly discomforted. Anyway, the rest of the evening was pleasant enough and ended with a mutual agreement for us to spend a few days together away somewhere, the Lakes possibly, or Cornwall. We didn't settle on the locality then and there, but the following day Vernon rang up suggesting of all places, Llanherrick.

'Why not?' he said when I prevaricated. 'The old hostelry's still there; I've got in touch, and it seems to me we couldn't find anywhere better. Good wining and dining, and fine country to explore. Remember?'

Oh yes, I remembered, including a few things I'd rather have forgotten; however Vernon was so insistent I eventually complied, having no logical excuse for refusal.

'Remember though,' I told him, 'no climbing tricky mountains. This time I want to enjoy the menu and scenery in peace. So it's valleys; understand?'

'Naturally,' he agreed after a perceptible pause.

Once the decision was taken I tried to put all niggling doubts aside, telling myself the unpleasant experience of those years ago had been merely the result of shock and pain combined with the weather and the unpleasant sense of being marooned on that remote mountain for an indefinite period. Vernon had said there *was* a chapel. Well, he was probably right, and my glimpse of the odd building a mere contortion of fact. I didn't allow the picture of the black-clad white-haired throng to gain precedence in my mind at that point, possibly I'd had a temperature and not known it which could have explained a macabre heightening of imagination; the brain could play strange tricks under certain conditions. What *did* concern me on the morning of our departure was my friend's repressed excitement which, despite all his efforts to appear calm, was obvious from his heightened colour and a certain brilliance in his eyes that didn't seem quite natural.

The mark too.

Time hadn't dimmed it at all. If anything it was clearer than before, reminding me of some Eastern caste mark, although I'd never seen one of such stark triangular design.

I found myself wishing I'd delved into a few books before starting off on this second jaunt; but the realm of ancient rituals, black magic, and hieroglyphics was an absorbing and lengthy study impossible to digest during the limited leisure hours of college life, and I'd certainly not counted on meeting up with Vernon again just at that time.

Anyway, when we reached the inn a good deal of my reluctance fell away. I'd forgotten how picturesque and truly ancient it was, and how admirably situated in its sheltered valley on the outskirts of the hamlet, Llanherrick. It stood facing three lanes ... one cutting back along a high moorland road to the small town of Brynna seven miles away, another dipping down into a wooded valley winding below the mountains towards Tywarth. The other ... well, as I didn't intend to go that way there was no point in considering it. So I dismissed it, concentrating instead on the thought of the good meal ahead.

And it *was* good. Plentiful and admirably cooked.

'Your choice of the place was right after all,' I told Vernon over drinks in the bar later. 'First rate in fact.'

'Thanks,' he said drily.

'And the bedrooms are pleasant,' I continued, 'at least mine is; far better than last time. I shall sleep like a log tonight.'

'Good.'

'Come on,' I said, trying to jerk him to some enthusiasm; after all he'd chosen to go there, 'What's wrong? If you want to switch your room for mine you're welcome.'

He jerked himself to attention, giving a quick smile that didn't somehow seem quite genuine.

'Oh no, *no*,' he said with more emphasis than was necessary. 'Sorry, Andy. I was just thinking.'

'What about?'

He didn't answer, and I gave up prodding; but the niggling idea occurred that he just might be remembering the distasteful episode of our previous visit. However that was his

202

affair, and I was determined not to let it impinge on my own self satisfaction.

We turned in early, and as I'd anticipated I went off to sleep almost immediately, and didn't stir until some hours had passed. When I woke it was with a start, and at first I didn't realise why. I switched on the lamp and looked at my watch. Two o'clock. God! what an hour to be disturbed. There was no wind either, no sound of a door rattling, or even squawking of a bird from outside. No jarring note at all, until ... my spine gradually froze as I heard it ... the long drawn-out tolling of a bell which gathered impetus as my ears became alerted to its mournful rhythm. And with every note memory of its sinister impact registered with eerie clarity, and I was once more picturing the procession of white-faced white-haired beings moving in a sombre dark-clad file to the luminous rectangular building waiting to receive them. The remembered mounting horror of the incident held me rigid, in a state of shock, as I recalled the leader turning and touching Vernon on the forehead, the brief pause before he started off again, a taller figure than the rest, and therefore more sinister in his dragging black robes.

If I'd had the courage I'd have got from my bed and gone to the window, but nerves, and a sudden blinding headache as though a sword had pierced my brain, held me static there, while the doleful tolling went on, holding the morbid note of a requiem to the dead. I knew though, without being told, or the evidence of my eyes that the air was thick outside, and heavy with yellow fog, and that in the awful valley below Hellescarne, the ghostly congregation would be filing into its grotesque temple of worship.

And Vernon?

I had a momentary impulse to go to his room, but when I tried to move my legs it was as though all mobility was frozen, and I fell back helplessly, closing my eyes, in a desperate effort for oblivion. For some time it was no use. An hour or more must have passed before the dismal tolling ceased. Then at last I fell into a fitful doze, hovering halfway between sleep and consciousness until the first signs of daylight penetrated the curtains.

I was properly woken by the girl with a morning cup of tea, which I drank loaded plentifully with sugar. This made me feel better, and I began to wonder if I'd dreamed about the bell. Some say nightmares are merely distorted impressions of previous happenings, and I'd certainly had thoughts in my mind about the strange affair when I went to bed, however hard I'd tried to repress them.

So optimistically reinforced by common-sense and the tempting odours of breakfast from below I presently got up, dressed, and went downstairs to the dining-room.

The two or three guests stopping there were already seated with coffee or tea before them. The tables were small and arranged attractively to catch the first glow of the morning sun, with a fine view of the countryside through the eastern window.

I was surprised not to see Vernon down; he was generally an early bird; but thinking he might have gone for a morning walk I ordered bacon and eggs and coffee and settled myself to enjoy a solitary meal. When I'd finished and he still hadn't appeared, I went upstairs to see if he'd overslept. But the room was empty. He'd obviously got up, dressed, and gone out. The bed was open with his night things thrown carelessly on the crumpled sheets, his windcheater wasn't on the peg or in the wardrobe. His outdoor shoes were nowhere about. Quite clearly he'd taken off somewhere at an ungodly hour when no one was about.

Puzzled I went downstairs and asked mine host as casually as possible if he'd seen my friend.

'No,' he said. He'd been up early, and as far as he was aware the gentleman hadn't been about. With the girl it was the same. Apparently Vernon hadn't replied when she'd knocked with his morning tea, and at nine o'clock it was still outside his room so she'd taken it down again.

After that I began to get worried. Creeping insidious fears grew in me when I recalled the sinister tolling of the night. I wished I'd got up and gone along to his room. He could have heard it too and taken off in the darkness for that weird place beneath Hellescarne, to meet and mingle with the unholy throng. I think I *knew* then that no part of that nightmare occasion those years ago had been hallucination. I'd *tried* to think so, but underneath, all the time, I'd known deep down, we'd both been witness to something not intended or good for human sight.

By ten-thirty, despite revulsion at the thought of returning, I decided to go and look for him. But before setting off I asked the landlord the name of the chapel or church lying near the foot of the mountain up the Llanherrick lane.

He looked puzzled.

'Chapel, sir? There's no chapel or church within ten miles of here except the one in the village itself.'

'A curious looking granite building?' I insisted, 'with an odd looking square tower. We got fog bound on the mountain the last time we were here, if you remember?'

'Oh yes. I remember that all right. The time you broke your leg.'

'Yes. Well, as we came down we passed the place. It *was* very misty of course, and...'

'You must have made a mistake, sir!' The man said quite decisively. 'There's *no* building that way. None at all, not for miles and miles.'

206

Although I'd half expected it, his words didn't help, and when I set off it was with a desolate sense of doom in me ... a queer inevitable feeling that if I *did* find Vernon it would be too late.

It was.

He was lying beneath the mountain in the exact spot I'd visualised—I recognised it from the pale granite stones, standing as grim sentinels over the forlorn terrain—but there was no chapel, no church, no tower or bell to toll its requiem for the doomed, only sparse turf and tumbled rocks bordered by a leafless tangle of furze and thorn straggling in black file by the edge of the lane.

And Vernon of course.

Vernon lying quite dead staring glassy-eyed towards the sky, his greenish white face just tipped with a film of gold from the lifting sun. I touched his hands; they were stiff and icy cold. Most probably he had died hours before. Some time in the night.

But after the first shock one thing registered above the rest. The mark on his forehead was no longer there.

And then I knew.

I was about to move away when I noticed something white lying near his side, a small thing, just a screwed up piece of paper with some writing on it—Vernon's.

Automatically I picked it up, and though the words were badly scrawled I could just decipher their meaning.

'Andy...' it read, 'The time has come. They have claimed me. Don't fret old chap. I knew it before. It was all writ. Borrowed time, old friend, borrowed time...'

There was no signature; clearly he'd had no strength to finish. I pushed the note into my pocket, but before I reached the inn again I took my lighter, flicked it to a sharp flame, and burned the paper till blackened embers were lifted like small dark ghosts into the air where they finally disintegrated and disappeared.

The reason given for his death was natural causes due to heart failure.

I couldn't quarrel with it, only wonder why Vernon, of all people, should have been chosen as one of the 'doomed'.

For doomed he had been, and he had known it.

As for the rest... well, I try now not to think of it. Naturally I have never since been within many miles of Hellescarne, and I know I never will again.

But at times still I am haunted by the memory of a dark valley with a bell tolling, and a procession of white-haired black-clad beings moving mournfully in single file to a pale temple no more seen.

CHAPTER THIRTEEN

TIME-SLIP

All that week I'd been a day earlier in my mind. Do you know what I mean? A queer sort of feeling that Tuesday was Wednesday, Wednesday Thursday, and so on. There seemed no particular reason for it, except that being early autumn there was that sort of dreaminess in the air that makes living a rather hazy affair ... a period for looking ahead and backwards at the same time so that it's easy to get lost in it. *Time*, I mean. Probably I'm explaining things very badly, but that's how it was with me for those strange few days.

Often I'd have to look at the paper to see the date; and generally I'd been wrong in my calculation. Odd really, considering what happened; and because it all amounted to such a mundane ordinary affair, ... my fortnightly visit to the hairdresser's.

When I was a girl I never bothered about a hairdresser's at all; but with the forties rushing headlong to the fifties, I'd seen through the mirror one day that 'tempus fugit' needed a bit of proper respect unless I was to turn into a real dowd ... you know, the on-the-shelf kind of spinster no man in his senses would give a second glance. Until that day the truth hadn't properly hit me. I wasn't bad looking, with a slim figure, looking far younger than my years, and able still, in the half light, to get an occasional wolf whistle from some passing male mildly in his cups. I should have guessed earlier of course, what was happening. Any woman in her senses should know that when tradesmen, or strangers for that matter, start addressing her as 'madam' instead of 'miss', it's 'goodbye to all that' ... romantically, and in any obvious sense.

It had been a bit of a shock to me at the start. *Other* women might develop small tell-tale lines and sagging neck contours, threads of grey ... although my hair was really rather good, ... but somehow you don't put yourself in that category until, as I've said, the truth shatters you one unsuspecting moment through 'the mirror'; then, naturally something has to be done about it.

So I'd started having my hair regularly shampooed, styled and set, with a professional colour rinse to emphasise those high-lights which are so frequently referred to in the glamour television adverts.

I'm explaining all this just to refute any suggestion that the 'time-slip' was due to some senile aberration of old age ... and God! how I hate those condescending individuals who seem to consider anyone over the sixty mark in need of patronage and sympathetic understanding ... but to show in the normal way I was capable of facing the truth.

The 'day ahead' business was an isolated incident which makes the whole episode so much more traumatic and significant.

My usual appointment was, and is, for 3.45 on Friday. And as usual, I caught the bus landing me at the square a quarter of an hour earlier, giving me ample time to walk the distance to the salon which was about half a mile.

Everything seemed unusually quiet that day. The shops leading towards the centre were generally buzzing with housewives and part-time career women like me, wanting to get extra bread and other groceries in ready for the weekend. But most of the doors were closed; a queer sense of apprehension seemed to hug the roof-tops with a pall of silence from the yellowing sky, creeping insidiously down alleys and thoroughfares where no one or nothing moved except the lean dark shape of a cat darting down an entry. I walked on, puzzled, and then, to my astonishment, saw the notice CLOSED on the door of a super-market. The next shop, a draper's, was just the same and the next and the next. Suddenly something clicked in my brain. I took out the little diary I carried in my handbag, studied it, and though thoroughly annoyed with myself, saw, with relief, that I'd made a mistake, fallen into the trap that had been dogging me all that week. It was a *Thursday*, half closing day. Not Friday at all. By then, near the busy part of the town, a certain amount of traffic was on the move, but it seemed to me more muted than usual. I had an odd off-beat sensation of trespassing where I shouldn't have, just at that moment. Maybe I paused for a second; I think I must have, because before reaching the turn, I was aware of a man staring down at me. He had a pleasant face, the kind of person, I knew instantly, I'd always hoped to meet, but never had ... rugged, middle aged, but sensitive, with very blue eyes and a touch of whimsical speculation about the well-cut lips.

He smiled briefly, sending a glow of warmth through my whole being. I wished I knew him; wished irrationally I could think up some excuse for making contact; asking the way somewhere, or pretending I'd lost a handbag or purse, and 'can you tell me, please, where the Police Station is?'

But of course this was quite ridiculous; and anyway wouldn't have worked, because I was never any good at lying. So before I hardly knew it, he'd gone on, and I was round the corner, in the street where the salon was cramped between two tall buildings, half way down. I'd got almost there, hoping it was open and they'd fit me in, when, with a terrific acceleration of sound, a car swooped down the road behind me, at such a speed I had to duck sharply into a doorway or I'd have been hit.

I waited in a daze for a second, because I was

212

really shaken. And then, suddenly, I heard it; a terrific grinding of brakes, and a high pitched scream. A girl or woman's. With nauseous terror I saw a body, wearing a blue coat exactly the shade of my own, caught and hurled into the air before the wheels went over it, crushing, grinding, and then, after a pause while I shut my eyes, suddenly started up again, with the car racing ahead until it disappeared round the next bend.

For a few moments I couldn't move. I just stood, temporarily stunned, praying someone would be on the scene before me. But the light had darkened ominously as though predictive of thunder, and nothing was clear any more. So I forced my limbs to action, and after the first dragging start, rushed and ran to the scene of the accident.

There was nothing there.

No sign of a body or tyre marks. And yet I had *seen* it; witnessed the whole thing. Was I going mad? Had I imagined the whole terrible incident? Or was it that during the brief interim I'd looked away, the body had been dragged into the car, and the wild hit-and-run driver, probably a drunk, taken a chance and speeded off without being noticed.

Reason told me this *must* be the answer, however improbable. Ought I to report it to the police? But without tangible evidence they'd never believe me; simply assume I was an hysterical female wanting attention, however

213

deviously contrived.

So I did nothing. And presently the normal sounds of traffic began to register. It was then I noticed the man I'd met earlier coming towards me again, his figure a little blurred in the uncertain autumn light.

Surely, I thought, he must have seen something, having come round the square by chance, to encounter me again in a perfectly haphazard meeting. On the way he was bound to have noted the car's abnormal speed. There was no other route for it to take.

I waited, with my heart pounding, for him to speak. He didn't: just smiled faintly but warmly, and went on again.

With a sense of dejection and helpless bewilderment, I went back to the hairdresser's, which I found, thankfully, open. Luckily for me there'd been a cancellation, which meant that I could be fitted in with my usual girl to do the snipping and setting.

I must have looked strange or something, because she said when I was properly settled in the chair with the white overall thing tied securely at the back to prevent any hair escaping down my neck, 'Are you all right, Miss Anstey?' There was concern in her voice. She seemed mildly troubled.

'Yes. Of course,' I answered, with an effort to sound bright. 'What makes you ask? Oh, I know I seem a bit het up. It's with making such a fool of myself; I mean coming in on the wrong day ... so stupid of me...'

I was on the point of confiding my unfortunate experience, but thought better of it. She'd probably not heard anything herself, if she had she'd have said something, and anyway there'd already have been police on the scene.

I couldn't understand it. The screams! The car's roar ... surely *someone*, somebody else besides me must have been about at the time. On the other hand the street *had* been extremely quiet at the time; I recalled, with a growing sense of unreality ... almost foreboding ... the yellow overhung sky, the emptiness for that brief time of normal traffic activity and pedestrians passing, except, of course, for the one stranger.

As I sat under the dryer with the girl busy with another client, I was angry with myself for having made no contact. I could have spoken; perhaps even if I'd said 'Good afternoon', or something trite like that, he'd have responded. But I wasn't the sort of female to make overtures to a man; and anyway, if he'd really wanted to speak to me he could have done so.

It was all very confusing, even a little frightening, and when I left the shop to catch the bus home an hour later, I felt more like something from *The Wizard of Oz* wandering by mistake through a bizarre world of make-believe, than flesh-and-blood Carrie Anstey, half expecting to see macabre cardboard

215

figures lurch out from the twilight. Well, twilight was hardly the proper term to describe the funny half-dark which had changed from thundery yellow to a cloying sepia-tinged mist. As I reached the bus stop, the air was heavy with the dead damp smell of tumbled leaves in suburban front gardens. People passed with faces tucked into their collars. Traffic droned from the distant main street and I shivered, not only from the sudden chill, but from the memory of that helpless blue-coated figure tossed into the air again and down under the car's wheels.

All that evening I couldn't get the picture out of my mind. But I was so tired I slept well, and in the morning decided that I'd make my usual jaunt into town as it *was* a Friday this time ... I checked by the calendar ... which meant the stores would be open for shopping.

What made me take the local train, I've no clear idea, except that it would be a change, even though it got into town half an hour later than the bus. Probably that was the main reason, as I'd already had my hair done, and shopping for one person didn't take all that long.

The weather was better than the previous day, with a radiance of pale sunlight filtering through veiled cloud. As before though, there was a queer lingering sense of something being odd, slightly out of key; a feeling that I'd lived this day already; was on my way along the inevitable course of cause-and-effect, of predestiny that couldn't be defined by any human element. I didn't particularly like it, and involuntarily quickened my pace from the station, walking instinctively I suppose towards the usual route leading to the salon.

I had just turned the corner when I saw it; an ambulance drawn up at the very spot of the accident the afternoon before. And something was being lifted inside. Something crushed and covered by a blanket ... face, everything; except for one hand dangling limply from a blue sleeve stained by blood.

A small crowd of sightseers was huddled closely into a doorway. There was the sudden drawn out wail of the siren as the vehicle started up, and sped purposefully in the direction of the hospital. But I knew, without having to be told, there was no true need for speed. The victim was dead; the victim in the blue coat, who could have been me, if I'd gone to the hairdresser's on my proper day, Friday.

'Oh yes,' a woman told me, when I reached the scene of the tragedy. 'She was killed outright. Not much left of her, poor thing. As for her face...' she shuddered. 'There wasn't any. That driver ... that devil! ... he should be made to pay. Put away for life he should be. Came round the corner and along like a mad thing he did, swerved, and got her straight in the back, tossed her up like a bag of feathers, then drove straight over her, poor thing, and got clean away. They'll get him though. *You see.*'

I knew though, that they never would, just as I knew when I felt a gentle touch on my arm, who it was.

'Come along,' he said gently. 'Let me take you somewhere; tea … or a drink perhaps. You've had a shock, haven't you?'

I looked up. The stranger's eyes, so very blue, were on my face compassionately. And although I didn't understand, I was aware, beyond all reason and logic that a power greater than human destiny had somehow stepped in to change a pre-ordained pattern into something else. Something belonging to the unchartered spheres of spiritual understanding, inviolate from human blundering.

The victim of the crash was never identified, and only one relic was retrieved as a clue … an Eastern type ring of the type found in countless boutiques these days. It was not claimed, and to have admitted that I had found my own identical one missing from my finger the previous afternoon, when I returned from the hairdresser's, might only have complicated matters. So I held my tongue. After all, no one would have believed the truth; … except, perhaps, Mark, who knew.

Since our marriage, which is usually happy, we have not mentioned the matter, or tried to solve the unsolvable. Some things are best left to sleep in that vast dream beyond the dream of ourselves and our own human existence. The miracle is that we found each other.

The rest, whilst we live, is immaterial.

CHAPTER FOURTEEN

TODD'S

It was only when he neared the house that the whispering began; ... a sibilant undertone of sighing, and murmuring and laughter, caught up by a whining wind where before everything had been still and silent. There would be a stirring in the grass and heather; an almost imperceptible quiver of undergrowth which for a moment sent a chill down his spine, combined with an irrational desire to plunge through the tumbled iron gateway and crumbling front door into the very recess of the building. But he resisted, and went hurrying past, remembering what the doctor had said, 'If you get any queer fancies while you're away, put them down and get them out of your system. Then take a stiff walk in the fresh air. Don't brood. You're better now, and in a week or two you'll be a perfectly fit man.'

He'd tried to believe it. But breakdowns weren't easy things to combat, and the trouble was as soon as he made an effort to get an idea on to paper, the irritation and nagging in his mind began ... the dull realisation of accepting that he was a failure and that the public and powers that were simply wouldn't accept him, except on a small scale, or give him an iota of

221

his literary due. Luckily he had means. But when a man was approaching fifty, with two marriages already on the rocks behind him and no children, the ego demanded more than a capacity to get through without financial worry.

To put his stamp on the world. Create something that mattered and won true acclaim! This was the dark demon that had driven him to hospital and six months' psychiatric care, ... this the haunting shadow still lingering somewhere at the back of his mind, though mostly now, he was unaware of it.

At first he'd thought the prolonged stay in Cornwall would completely work the trick. They were a jolly crowd at the farm and the food was excellent. For a week or two he'd been able to forget defeat and nervous torment, the sinister depression that no drugs had been able to alleviate. The farm, Trencarne, stood near the high moorland road leading to Porthzakka, three miles away; sufficiently remote to be peaceful, yet near enough to the small fishing town for company and shops when he felt like it. He was in good physical trim, and took a ramble most days, either down to the cove, or up the slope to the moor's summit behind, where the cromlech stood, a peculiar landmark of ancient stones, with a vista of the Atlantic below the distant cliffs.

222

The weather was fine, air heady with the mingled tang of fallen blackberries, dead leaves, damp undergrowth, and insidious drifting wood-smoke. He felt refreshed and invigorated, nostalgically aware not only of past youth, but of the pulsing of spring ahead already stirring the earth, … decay and new birth hand in hand urging him to a fresh future.

'I'll make it yet,' he thought frequently. 'Dammit … I'm still young enough to have a hell of a lot before me.' And he started planning, thinking of the next book he'd write, evolving an unusual plot which he was convinced would make the grade at last.

Then … one afternoon, he saw the house.

There was nothing unusual about it, except its unexpectedness, standing as it did on the side of a rough track half hidden by undergrowth, which until then he'd not stumbled across. It was grey, square-faced, with an overgrown path leading from broken iron gates to a Georgian porticoed entrance. A neglected dwelling, obviously empty, with blank windows staring like sightless eyes from granite walls encrusted with ivy.

No sight or sound of movement anywhere, not even the scurry of a small wild thing, flutter of a bird, or a sheep or cow grazing in adjoining fields. Yet the very air seemed filled with threatening uneasy life, as though by chance he'd strayed into another dimension waiting for recognition. And almost instantaneously a shiver of wind stirred the bushes and bracken. He fancied for a moment a light flashed and died behind one of the windows, while the whispering started ... sly, hardly more than a stirring of the elements, but punctuated by baleful obscene chuckles of amusement emitting a curious invidious power.

He stood perfectly still for a brief pause, sensing a powerful magnetic urge to enter, while the damp air curdled automation and will into useless negation. Then, with desperate incentive, salvaging sanity from evil compulsion, he forced himself ahead and at running speed passed the desolate domain until he reached a terrain of safety twenty yards or so further on, where the view quietened once more into the silent serenity of a perfectly normal afternoon, with dying sunlight touching the gnarled twisted sloes and thorn trees to pale gold, spreading its film over gorse, heather, and silent small fields sloping to the sea.

After such a nasty experience he determined never to go that way again.

But he did.

It was as though he had to discover for himself where reality ended and imagination began ... the meeting point of two spheres perhaps or even two times ... which could exist alongside each other, with the darker always waiting to encroach upon the normal, given favourable emotional and elemental conditions.

Once he said to the farmer's wife, 'That house ... the one shut away off the lane down a track ... it's very overgrown; you must know it...' He attempted to describe its situation exactly, ending as nonchalantly as possible ... 'Obviously it's empty. I wondered why. It looked a reasonable property, or *could* be, with a bit of repair and modernizing.'

The woman stared at him contemplatively for a moment then turned away saying, 'I think I know the place you mean, Todd's. Yes. It's been empty for more years than I can remember. The land's not good there. Some say...' her voice trailed off.

'Yes?'

'Oh...' she shrugged. 'Foundations not supposed to be good I've heard. Dry rot. Too cut off anyway. And there are mine shafts about, all sorts of dangers. Bog, too. Folk've gone round in the past, more than one, and never been seen since. Locals don't like it. Well, I don't blame them. And if I were you, Mr Sheldon, I'd steer clear of that bit of ground.'

'Perhaps you're right,' he agreed.

But right or wrong made no difference. Inevitably, as the days passed, he found himself wandering automatically in the direction of the desolate house,—or maybe 'terrain' described it better—where he'd pause briefly before taking the first step towards the tumbled gates. Once in its malevolent aura, he'd feel horror emanating from the air, ground, and most of all from the gaping doorway of Todd's, a force so evil, sickness would rise in him momentarily, and his limbs tremble until with a tremendous effort he'd somehow manage to move and bluster on, head thrust forward, hands outstretched defensively, though no physical barrier materialised, only foul lurking menace gathering into a huge wave of obscene elemental power.

Then it would be over.

He'd pause breathlessly, turn and stand there, seeing nothing but the humped shape of a building squatting in clumps of twisted trees, windows blank and sightless, like great eyes with lids fallen over them shutting out life and any lurking movement within.

By the time he came to a turn cutting abruptly backwards up the lane, reaching the point he'd started from, forming a kind of triangle, the view, on looking back, would appear perfectly static and normal; just a vista of empty moorland interspersed with small fields and occasional clumps of trees from which a tip of a chimney emerged, unnoticeable except to anyone knowing it was there.

Yet every time he went that way it was the same—fear, sudden panic on reaching the house, followed by a wild need to drag his feet to rushing speed, until he was once more on safe ground. And instead of abating, his neurosis seemed to increase. By then he'd accepted it *was* a neurosis, and that he was not as well as he'd thought he'd been.

There was only one course therefore: to face the illusion, aberration, or whatever it was, squarely, so that it remained no longer a compulsion in his mind, but could be obliterated for good.

The day was motionless, filled with the radiance of sunlight when he set off one afternoon with nerves and body steeled for action.

Cutting down the lane he was vaguely aware of the intermittent chirrup of a bird and occasional drift of a leaf falling from a tree, the crackle and rustle of twigs under-foot, and the brush of narrowing hedges as he reached the track and turned. Otherwise all was silent, holding a dream-like quality giving no indication of impending menace; no threat or sense of doom, until a wall appeared half-submerged by trees.

He went on automatically, feet slowing to a grudging pace, eyes fixed on the looming boxlike erection of granite that presently stood clearly defined where the track turned.

Empty windows gaped and stared.

The hole of a door quivered fleetingly in the fitful afternoon light, stretching into the semblance of a senile grin as a shadow passed, subtly, sickeningly inviting. Or was it merely his fancy?

He stood for a second or two, tensing himself to meet the challenge before approaching the iron gates deliberately, though his heart lurched.

The atmosphere became increasingly malevolent, sucking his impetus into a furry negation of non-resistance; the air was thick and cloying, choking his throat, and encircling his body as though coils of greedy etheric fog crept purposefully from the interior of the building seeking to entrap him.

He lifted his hands automatically before his face, and contacted ... nothing. But at the same time a chortle of sinister laughter resounded against his ear-drums, followed by the insidious impression of stirring and whispering. The earth and air seemed to curdle into one, shifting a little under his feet; and as he blundered past the broken iron leading to the entrance, a flash of light struck sideways from a jagged window frame, lifting the whole scene briefly to contorted baleful clarity. There was a sudden pounding and roaring behind him. He turned sharply to see something with great horns rushing through the undergrowth, wide mouth agape, reddened eyes pin-points of evil.

He lurched ahead running blindly into the dark hall, which was dank and foul-smelling from damp, decay and droppings of bats encrusting the cobwebbed ceiling and floor flags.

He slumped to the ground and sat with his back against the cold wall while the whispering started up again, intermingled with a movement of the darkness into shadowy forms and faces of unspeakable malignancy, caricatures of humanity, loose-lipped and lascivious, greedy covetous hands touching and seeking his flesh, lit to passing clarity by a blaze of jewels, of thrusting naked female breasts where diamonds glowed incongruously through the macabre setting, and slit-eyed immense male visages leered about and around him, tweeking his ears and clothing, mouthing obscenities followed by a rising crescendo of soulless derisive laughter.

The walls seemed to converge and close in on him, while innumerable sucking lips pressed and expanded on his face, drawing the breath and lifeblood out of him.

With a superhuman effort he succeeded in propelling himself to his feet, one hand at his throat choking for air, before managing at last to extricate himself and feel the door.

He plunged through, and a moment later was lying on the tangled path outside, briars and twisted sloes crouched round him, a few last leaves floating down from the branches of a sycamore above. The air had quietened, lying cool on his face.

But it was too late.

A farmer found his body the next day, when

he'd gone in search of a wandering cow; never, he told his cronies later had he seen such a terror on any man's face before! The animal also, which he discovered lying at the back of the house was dead, eyes open and glaring, tongue caught between its teeth. The cause of death in both cases was said afterwards to be from heart failure due to extreme shock; possibly from lightning, as thunder was about that day. But no one in the district really accepted the explanation, the general verdict being that the authorities were ignorant about the land round Todd's.

Rumours and conjectures were whispered from mouth to mouth; hints of haunting and evil spells; others of a more material calibre, suggesting bad gases leaking from some unknown source; of faulty terrain from forgotten underground mine-workings which could shift under certain elemental conditions, with frightening impact, accounting for the strange fact that no beast or bird generally strayed into the immediate vicinity.

But no one *knew*; although a local 'ancient' who remembered the late owner of the house had another theory.

'*Power*,' he muttered, the following evening over his pint in The Fisherman's Arms. 'That was it. Sick for et he was ... Abraham Todd. A real devil's miser ... power o' gold an' lustin' flesh; to have his fist on all he did meet, beast or man, or chile or wumman. None was safe from

230

'en, an' such as he doan' sleep o' nights nor rest in peace. No grave can hold 'en. Should be burned down, that's what I do say, ... Todd's should be burned, every stick an' stone of et; so 'twill be, one day.'

And it was.

By whom it was never discovered, and the authorities were not too much perturbed. No one wanted the property. It was an eye-sore anyway, and the land best left to Nature's refurbishing.

This occurred eventually, though little grew there but straggling weeds waving thin arms covetously to the sky, interspersed with clutching thorn and the crouching humped heads of yellow fungi massed together as though in whispering evil commune.

CHAPTER FIFTEEN

HAVEN'T WE MET BEFORE?

From the first moment she felt ill-at-ease in the large bedroom, and wished she had obeyed her instinct to refuse the Christmas invitation to Carnwikka. 'Do come,' the school friend of her youth had written. 'A week's break will help you get over your mother's death, and it will be fun talking over old times, won't it? It's such an age since we met; eight years. Or is it more? And such a lot's happened...'

Yes, Ann Treen had thought, reading Phyllida's large scrawl. 'To you, perhaps. But not to me.'

This was true. Phyllida, with a rich husband, children, a town house and home in Cornwall, could have no conception what it had been like spending the best youthful years trying to cope with a sick and querulous widowed mother, and humdrum secretarial job at the same time: never known what real tiredness was ... the weariness of falling to sleep each night knowing that every day ahead would be the same, because there was no time for anything else ... parties, fun, or having men friends. Just work and strain. Now, although at thirty she was free at last to lead her own life, loneliness and fear engulfed her, because she did not

233

know where to begin.

Phyllida's invitation had come out of the blue. 'There'll be just a few friends,' she concluded. 'Two or three. No more. So don't go all shy like you used to be. This is a lovely old house converted of course, with a new wing. But you'll be crazy about it.'

After Ann's first hostile reaction, the idea had made sense. Now she was already regretting her acceptance. As she'd passed through the hall up the stairs she'd realised with a sinking of her heart that the 'few friends' were quite a large gathering ... smart and sophisticated or trendy and colourful people, and not her kind at all. They would be polite of course, but beneath the veneer would be pity. And pity, just then, was the last thing she wanted.

The bedroom was typically 'Phyllida', with expensive modern furnishing ... a violet coloured ceiling dotted with stars ... one blue wall, two cream, and a pink; there were switches and buttons everywhere, a private bathroom complete with shower and heated handrails. Everything for comfort, except the indefinable quality of being lived in, and perhaps, loved.

When the maid had left and the door been closed, Ann sat on the bed with a mounting feeling of confusion and unhappiness. The echo of voices drifted up from below, interspersed by the intermittent twanging of a guitar, and this, somehow, seemed wrong; out of key. She guessed that the room had been rebuilt on part of the original house, and wondered idly what the place had looked like in the old days. She could visualise ivory walls and rose-wood furnishings, velvet hangings and chandeliers or candles instead of the cunningly contrived wall lighting; yes, once Carnwikka could have been elegant yet comforting. She wished for a moment she had lived a century or two ago. Then, with an effort of will she got up, opened her case, took out her few clothes, laid her underwear in the chest, and hung her coat and costume in the wardrobe, leaving her one evening maxi dress on the bed.

When she'd had a wash and put the frock on, she went to the mirror and took a good look at herself. She had thought herself extravagant when she'd brought the violet shaded velvet. But it had seemed worth it. Now she had to face the fact it looked drab. She was too pale. Her shoulder-length hair was too mousy and lank. She had chosen the colour to emphasise the violet lights of her eyes, which were her best point. Now they seemed to have sunk into nondescript pools of shadows in her heart-shaped face. It would be the same story here as at the other rare social functions she had braved herself to endure, she thought. She would be unnoticed, ignored after the first few seconds of conversation ... the spinster wallflower, with the strained set smile on her lips, while men swarmed round other women flatteringly. Through the years she had almost come to believe that she didn't care. But she did. Always, secretly, she had longed for attention and affection. No one at the office had guessed, of course. But Ann, more than most women, had hoped desperately for a husband and family of her own. Perhaps if she'd not been so shy ... if her mother had not been so demanding ... but 'ifs' were a waste of time. She knew now that her potential capacity for affection would never have an outlet. She was one of the surplus kind.

Trying to shake off her depression, she got up, went to the window, drew the curtains and looked out. The film of sleet-like rain shivered against the glass, lit to glittering radiance from car lights below. At moments the whole scene became clear ... the wide drive and gracious lawns sloping to the estuary beyond. Then the shapes faded again into the general quivering dazzle of thin blown rain.

She went back to the mirror and noticed for the first time its beauty. This surely was the real thing; antique French, perhaps, with bevelled glass and oval gilt carved frame. A mirror to frame beauty. But she was not beautiful.

Then it happened.

Slowly, from the shadowed background, a face emerged behind her shoulder; dream-like, as though half-erased by time ... a woman's

236

face, gentle, wide-eyed with lips half parted expectantly, her silky light brown hair piled high on her head entwined with ribbon. She was wearing a violet gown, and was not alone. Behind her stood a man, his figure only half defined in the greyness, but with features lit for a single second into vivid clarity ... finely modelled, with a warm smile, and dark eyes searching, as though through the years. Ann stared, watching the girl turn momentarily towards him and draw his head down to hers. Seconds passed, minutes ... or more ... in that motionless interlude. But for the first time in her life Ann, in a rush of familiarity, knew the full anguish of envy and loss; knew that his was the face she'd pictured from early adolescence; knew too that his love was for the woman in the mirror world; that they were united in a region beyond space and time. What were they then; and who and what was she?

Question after question flooded her mind as she struggled for some straw of reality. Facts, only half registered, slowly came into place, bringing a quickening of her heart and a sudden trembling to her whole body. She tried to move, but couldn't. Then a wave of giddiness forced her automatically to a chair where she sat with head slumped into her hands until the faintness had passed.

When she had recovered sufficiently to force herself to the mirror again, it was her own face staring back at her ... the colourless face of plain Ann Treen, with her fine hair falling on either side ... hair without a wave or life which did nothing for her.

But if she put it up? If she dared to tie it with the scrap of ribbon she'd brought in case she needed it?

Without pondering the question any further, she took pins and comb from her handbag, and the next moment was lifting the silken weight of her fine hair in her hands. Instinctively she coiled it in tendrils on top of her head, threading it with the lilac ribbon. At first she could hardly believe the reflection before her was that of the mundane young woman no man had wanted or cared for. This girl was lovely in a fawn-like way, desirable. As lovely as that other ... the one she'd imagined those few short minutes ago. As she loosened the neck of the purple velvet a little, she even persuaded herself for a fraction of time that the man was there, just slightly behind ... that he was no stranger. She had known him for ever; she must have done, in some other life.

Then, suddenly, her dream-like happiness changed to a slow welling-up of terror as the impression of his form became completely obscured by a creeping lurid glow of red light which quivered and deepened and turned into leaping flames. A choking smell of smoke curdled the room, thick and pungent, until nothing was visible but dense blackness, lit by intermittent vivid crimson.

Ann rushed to the window, flung it open, and saw, where the cars had stood, just a huddled crumbling shape which could have been of an arbour or barn and was already a blazing inferno of destruction driving towards the house. That was not all. On the fringe of the fire the figure of a man was struggling ineffectually to escape; a dark dot against the lurid light. Once, his voice thin and high, rose in a cry for help above the crackling roar of tumbling masonry. Ann rushed from the room screaming and calling as she ran down the stairs, pushing past the astonished crowd of people, along the wide corridor and out of the front door, racing down the steps towards the flames. He was still struggling when she reached him with her hands outspread, clutching his wrists ... dragging him and pulling ... from the vortex of terror and death. There was a choking in her throat; she could hardly breathe; but she knew he was there stumbling after her, could feel his hand in hers. When they reached the steps of the house, it happened. There was a sudden deafening roar with a blinding light which shattered her into forgetfulness. She fell. The last words she heard were, 'Thank God, Tony. Thank God.'

*   *   *

Then, mercifully, peace came.

When she recovered consciousness she was

239

in the bedroom with Phyllida standing by her. 'Oh Ann,' she heard her friend saying, 'Thank heaven you're all right. I mean ... if you'd been killed ... but how did you *know*? How on earth *could* you?'

'If you don't mind we'll leave the questions till a little later,' another voice voice said. 'Miss Treen's been through enough for the time being.'

Ann closed her eyes and slowly started remembering. Like the figments of a nightmare returned, she recalled the fire, the tormented figure ... his voice ... she looked up again. An elderly man, obviously a doctor was looking down on her handling a stethoscope and with him was someone else; someone who said with a faint smile on his lips, dark eyes searching hers, 'You've saved my life you know. That foul thing must have been planted in my car before I left town. But...' he paused questioningly, 'Haven't we met before?'

Moments passed before Ann answered quietly, 'Perhaps ... yes. We must have ... a long time ago...'

How long, or where, didn't really matter. Both knew that.

The link between them ... the strange inexplicable link ... was stronger than time and the passing of the centuries; and it was something more than chance which had driven Ann to accept Phyllida's invitation that Christmas. No one understood, of course, certainly not the police, when they asked her how she knew there was a bomb in Tony Grant's car, one of those evil planned outrages of a current sick society. 'I didn't,' she said. 'It was just flames I saw; through the mirror first, then I looked out of the window and there was the fire.'

'But Ann dear, there was *no* fire,' Phyllida remarked firmly. 'We'd have known; we were in the hall ... there was only that icy rain. Then suddenly there you were, clutching at Tony who was just locking his car.'

'True enough,' the inspector confirmed. 'The blast didn't happen until you were both back at the house.'

'Then ...' Ann shook her head slowly. 'I was very tired of course. I'd been under a strain. My mother had died ... and perhaps ... perhaps I'd been dreaming.'

Her explanation was accepted. It had to be. Although as Phyllida pointed out later there was one queer coincidence about the whole thing. 'Carnwikka was half destroyed by the Roundheads in Cromwell's era,' she said. 'I was reading about it recently in an old book. There's a legend supposed to be true ... a sad sort of tale ...'

'Tell me,' Ann urged.

'The daughter of the house, a very beautiful girl, was to be married the following day. But she and her lover both died in the flames. She tried to rescue him, but it was no good. That's why her ghost's supposed to haunt the house, always looking for him ...'

When Ann said nothing she went on, 'Funny isn't it ...?'

'What?'

'That mirror in your bedroom ... it's very old. Probably belonged to her. We bought it with the house and a few other special pieces.'

'I'm glad you did,' Ann said very quietly.

'You don't mind then? You don't want it taken away? Because of the ghost, I mean.'

Ann smiled gently. 'I don't think any ghost here will walk again,' she replied with quiet conviction.

The next Christmas, following her marriage to Tony Grant, they visited Phyllida once more.

The mirror was still there.

A beautiful but perfectly normal mirror, reflecting just two young people very much in love and looking ahead to the future in vindication of the bitter past.

CHAPTER SIXTEEN

THE CIRCLE

It was evening when I came to the inn, and a mist crept up from the sea like a shroud to the cliffs and gaunt hills beyond. From my first glimpse I knew instinctively it was not a good place. Yet I knew, too, that I should stay. There *are* places like that. Once in a lifetime perhaps most of us have the experience—a clutch of the heart, a familiarity, a sense of belonging—though the district is alien and strange. Yet I hope most fervently there are few who go through what I went through at Trendragon.

I was recuperating from a breakdown in health, and on my doctor's orders had been walking for a week. Therefore, perhaps, my nerves at that time were abnormally sensitive to impressions and suggestions. I was possibly nearer to the occult world than a man in normal health would have been. That may be. But the fact remains—I knew Trendragon was a bad place. I knew it, and yet I stayed. It was as though in those first brief moments the sinister country laid its hand upon me, impelling me through the doorway into the hall of that isolated pub where a few countrymen were gathered in the draughty lamplight drinking

243

their beer and playing darts.

There was a woman serving in the bar; a woman with a pale face and black hair that had a hint of red in it. Her lips were red too; full, and arrogantly curved. I didn't like her, but she smiled at me, and when I asked her for a bed, made arrangements for me to stay with a veneer of politeness and welcome. Beneath her pleasantries, however, I sensed hostility. Her father, the landlord, was hostile too. Oh no, he didn't say anything. Nothing that could be taken amiss. But he watched me; it seemed to me that the whole place watched. Each time I went to the bar there was a hush in the conversation, a withdrawing and suspicious silence, which told me they were against me more strongly than any open avowal could have done.

It was a queer feeling—that sense of being watched. And it was not only the people—it was in the air itself, in the very mist which crept insidiously through the cracks of the windows and doors, giving a dimness to everything, a chill and dampness which, despite the fire, pressed unpleasantly round the collar of my coat, brushing my face with the clammy touch of ghost fingers.

When I had had my supper of bread and cheese and ale the woman took me to my room.

'It's not large,' she said, 'but not many folk come here to stay. We don't cater for visitors.'

I saw before me a small room with a sloping

ceiling supported by beams. A dressing-table stood in one corner, with a candle on it, and in the other a side table holding a wash-basin. The bedstead was a lumbering four-poster affair. I could see nothing very distinctly, and the impression was one of encroaching gloom. I shivered on the threshold, hesitating, searching quickly through my mind for some excuse to go away again. But it did not come, and if it had I should not have taken it. I know that now. Some purpose linked me for that brief period to the draughty inn and primitive countryside; some purpose from the past, which was stronger than reason or common sense.

Oh, I know that on paper, in the light of daytime, all this must sound fantastic. But Cornwall is a strange country, and I was in that state of mind most receptive to queer conditions. When you have heard the rest of the tale you will, of course, judge for yourself.

Shortly afterwards the woman left me, and I was able to make a further examination of my surroundings. The curtains were drawn, but I went to the window and opened them. The mist had lifted a little, and before me I saw stretched the gaunt outline of a moorland hill rising to the greenish glow of the sky, its shape jagged and broken by rocks and the skeleton, dark silhouette of a ruined tin mine. And as I watched I was overcome by an unexplainable compelling sense of horror. All my foreboding was manifest suddenly in that stark outline, in its peak, which was surmounted by a most curious-looking stone, circular and hollowed out in the centre, surrounded by several perpendicular pillars. It was horrible. I did not know then *why* it was horrible; but it was. I closed the curtains with hands which trembled. The sweat was damp on my brow.

I chided myself for being a fool. My doctor would laugh at me, I told myself—a fit of the nerves again, no more. But my heart was beating heavily. I remembered tales I had heard of ancient rites, and the practice of black magic which had gone on from time to time in certain parts of Cornwall. Here, if anywhere, such things might occur.

That night I slept very little and was grateful when the morning came at last, bringing sunshine and comparative normality.

The woman brought me my breakfast into the parlour. I remember every detail of that parlour now, the sea-chest in one corner, the oleograph of the Battle of Trafalgar hanging over the old-fashioned mahogany sideboard, the glass case with a stuffed squirrel in it, and the aspidistra in a pink pot in the window. The room faced the opposite way to my bedroom, and I had a view of the cliffs and sea in the morning sunshine. The smell of the coffee from the kitchen was good. I should not have felt depressed, yet the intangible unpleasant aftermath of a bad nightmare persisted, overhanging and clouding everything with an insidious yellow quality.

The woman spoke in a forced, bright voice.

'Slept well?' she enquired briskly.

'Oh, not so bad for a first night,' I lied non-committally.

'It's good air here,' she said.

'Yes, I should imagine so. I'm looking forward to a decent walk.'

But I was conscious all the time that we were both playing parts, and that her eyes were vigilant, watching me, as though waiting for something.

I get on with most people. Generally I am not given to personal aversions. But there was something about that woman which repulsed me. Repulsed and yet haunted me. Something cruel and sadistic, which was epitomized in the country itself.

'Tell me,' I said, as she brought in the coffee, 'what's that stone on the top of the hill?'

I thought for a second she started, could sense a tension in the atmosphere, and saw her eyes narrow slightly before she answered casually:

'Oh, that! No one knows what it is. It's very old. No one goes there much.'

'*I* shall go,' I said, unexpectedly, even to myself.

'Hm! Well—it's queer country. You just be careful, sir.'

'Careful? What do you mean?'

She shrugged her shoulders.

'Mine-shafts,' she said. 'Bog. You just take care.'

It was a pretence of speaking on my behalf. But I knew she resented my enquiry. I knew she hated me for a few moments, as *I* hated her. I looked up, staring her straight in the face. With her white skin, red lips and black hair she had a wanton look. She repelled me; but I could feel my heart quicken. It was as though she held me ensnared. And I had an urge to shame her. Sensations I had not known struggled in me for expression. Bad feelings roused by bad things. I forced my eyes away, and heard her laugh, softly. Then she swung towards the door.

'Remember,' she said, 'I've warned you!'

Later I went out and, impelled by an impulse I could not battle against, cut up behind the inn towards the stones. As she had said, it was bad going. It was as if everything about that hill was bad. Bad and beautiful; and older and stronger than humanity. And yet I felt a kinship with it all, almost as though in some strange other life I had known it before—the rough track tangled with gorse and bracken, the tangy smell of bog and sea, the grey shapes of the rocks rising in primeval beast-like forms from the undergrowth, and the mounting sense of vitality which possessed me the higher I climbed. It was an exultant feeling; that feeling of ancient knowledge, tingling my blood-stream with lust and power. But there was dread there too, of that same force which held and drew me to the top.

There was no breath of wind when I got there, and everywhere was very quiet—so still that the scene might have been painted—the great circular erection outlined against the sun, with the five perpendicular satellite stones grouped round. All about me the warm autumn light quivered in a haze of heat. But as I waited a change took place. It seemed to me, incongruously, that the yellow of the bracken, the texture of the very stones, changed gradually to a creeping, deepening crimson. I rubbed my eyes, with a sense of horror chilling my blood. I wanted to scream, to move, anything to break the silence. But my feet felt chained by the earth I stood upon, while the crimson turned darker, to the colour of blood itself. Then, abruptly, it had faded, and the stones stood there as before, calm and grey under the sky.

I turned and ran, jumping and blundering down the hill-side, slipping and pulling myself up again; not pausing until I reached the track at the bottom leading to the inn. When I turned I saw the stone above me, round and stark, like some immense eye watching, exuding evil. I did not go in directly, but rested for some time until my nerves had steadied, and the sickness passed from my brain and stomach. Later, when I entered the parlour the girl was laying the table. And it was curious, the sight of her sturdy figure seemed to rouse odd half-formed memories in me; not of the present at all but of some other period beyond the limits of age and time. And when she turned her eyes upon me I knew she also was aware of it, and was experiencing the same emotion.

I well know that all this must sound fantastic—a neurotic fabrication of a sick mind. But it was more than that.

That night I slept no better. The moon was up, and though the curtains were drawn, its light penetrated the room with a pale, malevolent insistence which set my imagination racing, leaving me alert to every creak of the door and floor-boards, to every slight tap at the window, or chance wild crying of some passing sea bird.

At two o'clock I slipped into a fitful doze, and woke about an hour later, suddenly alive to the muffled sound of voices below. Shortly afterwards, only half aware of my actions, I got out of bed, lighted my candle, and opened my door, listening. I don't know what I expected to hear. But I was conscious of a danger more deadly than any open attack. I crept downstairs to the parlour, and what I saw at the foot of the stairs confirmed my suspicions. The door of the room was shut—and facing me, hanging there, was the sign of the black mass. Then I knew. I knew, indeed, that foul things went on at Trendragon.

In the morning I did not feel well, and

250

thought of leaving. But I did not; it was almost as though I *could not*.

A fortnight passed. And then one night when the man and his daughter had gone to bed I took a late stroll up the hill towards the fatal stone. There was a mist, but the moon was up, its pale light filtering the thin fog into strange wraith forms which curled and billowed about like dead things come to life. It was a night for the dead. A chill little wind moaned through the bracken and round the grey stones, flapping the moisture against my face, blowing through the black branches of the bushes which waved in thin, spectral shapes before my eyes. I do not know what I thought to find up there that night. But I knew the moment had come to face it.

The mist was thicker at the top, curling and writhing, snake-like, about the stones. My pulses thudded with apprehension as I drew nearer with trembling limbs, until I was close enough to touch its rough surface. Why I touched it, I cannot explain. But the contact caused me to shudder and draw back, with a wave of faintness upon me, which forced me to my knees there, head in hands. When I looked up again I saw in the distance the mist take shape, and forms appear through the greyness, drawing closer and closer, while I waited, too terrified to move. And I think I knew in that awful moment what was to come. I think, subconsciously, I had always known, and that

251

my vigil was but some re-enacted incident from an age far past, when something of me, perhaps, had undergone the same terror.

I tried to rise, but I could not. I stretched my arms unthinkingly to the stone for support, and as I did so I fell, with my head half through the circle. A scream came to my throat, but was stifled as the figures approached, larger now, more solid and real, surrounding the stones. They were tall, white-clad figures, wild-eyed and chanting, with some fixed ceremonial purpose which signified, I knew, my death.

I tried to tear myself from the stone, but there was no life in me. It was as if my body was chained there, until the dread ritual was performed. And as I waited it seemed to me that the fog lifted a little, and the light deepened to a reddish glow. I saw one figure—a man's—detach itself from the rest and step forward, his white robe and beard blowing in the mist as he lifted his arms wide to the heavens, giving some pagan cry which I did not understand.

After that many things happened; things which I cannot recall even now without nausea and shame. I think at one point I must have fainted. For when I came to myself the shadow of the stones had changed. The mist had gone, and the moon struck full on my upturned face.

And at that moment I saw a woman approaching me. She wore a white gown like the others, and her red hair fell loose about her shoulders. She stepped forward slowly, something held in her hand—a knife. Her red lips were fixed into a smile of sensuous cruelty, her black eyes narrowed in her pale face. She walked slowly, ceremoniously, like some high priestess about to pass sentence. And the smile on her lips was the death smile. Not *her* death—mine! I knew then that the stone on which I lay was a sacrificial altar, and that I was the sacrifice. I watched her, hypnotised by my own fear, as she drew nearer, ready at the sign, to strike. And as she lifted her arm her gown blew away from her throat, and I noticed quite a small thing about her—a minute triangular red mark on her right shoulder, near her neck.

The next moment there was a united wail from the other grouped figures, and in that instant something in me came alive, in protest not only against death but against the unholiness of the ritual.

As the knife was about to fall I was able to raise my right hand, crossing myself swiftly on the forehead and breast.

Then I waited, with my eyes closed.

When I opened them I saw, miraculously, the figures dissolving into the mist, becoming no more than half-formed shadows of cloud and fog, while the sky darkened and everything, mercifully, went from me.

It was morning when I came to myself again, and I was still lying with my body against the stone. I picked myself up, remembering with horror the night's events, looking round for some sign of the barbaric happenings. But there was none; all was solitary and quiet. Only the lonely hill under a grey sky, with the stone standing bleak and cold in the early light.

I turned and hurried down.

The girl was already about the house when I arrived. She looked tired with rims under her eyes. I wondered why I had ever thought her good-looking. She appeared then completely ordinary. Her power had gone but she looked at me strangely, almost furtively.

'You're early, sir,' she said, in a flat voice.

'Yes,' I replied, easily. 'I've been walking.'

I did not give any explanation; there was no need. But I told her I should be leaving after breakfast.

'I see,' she remarked. 'Oh!—all right!'

I knew she was disappointed about something. And I think I knew what.

Before I left she said to me:

'Perhaps you'll come again one day?'

'I think it most unlikely,' I said, steadily watching her. I noticed her flinch, draw back, almost imperceptively. I noticed something else too. The collar of her blouse had fallen back, and I saw there on her right shoulder, near the neck, a curious birthmark, shaped like a scarlet triangle.

CHAPTER SEVENTEEN

THE THINGUMMYJIG

She'd always been afraid, even as a child. Of the stiff-backed aunt who'd brought her up, her governess, the austere housekeeper with keys dangling on a chain from her waist, the dour cook, and the two elderly great-uncles who paid occasional visits to the large square house.

The house, Froggetts, stood close to a squelchy dark marsh. She was frightened of that too, with its sombre rooms, long dark corridors, and creakings of doors and floorboards. But most of all she feared great-grandfather.

He lived mostly in two rooms upstairs, and had become in her imagination the symbol of all evil that befell her ... an awesome ancient judge responsible for scoldings and whippings, ... though she seldom saw him ... looming always in the background, with the power at any moment of calling doom upon her.

The sound of his stick thumping on the sitting room ceiling struck terror into her heart and when her aunt said, 'If you dare do "this or that", I'll tell your grandfather,' her knees shook so much they nearly crumpled under her.

255

His appearance was grotesque; long white beard and whiskers covering a face so gnarled and old only the eyes seemed alive ... fierce beady eyes darting here and there under bristling brows, quicker than a snake's about to strike. At the rare times he came downstairs to greet his brothers when they called, he was propelled down by the man Joseph in a curious kind of chair, step by step, until he reached the hall, where he swivelled the thing round himself with annoying speed, head thrust forward from humped shoulders.

On such occasions Clarissa crept away quietly to avoid him as long as possible, until the inevitable tea-time when she was forced to sit at the immense mahogany white-spread table, with her fearsome elders around her. It was on one of these days that she first saw the Thingummyjig. That is ... *properly*. She'd half glimpsed him many times, once poking his head round a chimney-pot; at another watching her from a dark corner of her vast ugly bedroom where she'd been sent in disgrace, at others just slipping along the landing or behind the ponderous grandfather clock in the hall. He was small and round with large feet and hardly any legs at all, having no hair on his head, but wearing a peculiar kind of hat like a clown's.

He was generally smiling, and his smile reached from ear to ear, or *would* have if he had any. Actually there were none to be seen, so the effect was rather like a thin red line drawn in a curve across the surface of a huge turnip. Many children would have been scared. But Clarissa wasn't. Smiles were so rare in her life. So when she met him face to face by the arbour on an afternoon of her great-uncle's visit, she was relaxed suddenly, and smiled back.

After that they became friends, and gradually as the days passed, the little girl realised that the Thingummyjig was not only funny, but clever. When something nasty was going to happen he generally managed to appear and warn her. And if it was *very* bad, he could stretch himself from a ball into a long snake with such a frown on his face she was almost frightened herself.

It became an understanding between them that she never divulged his presence to the adults. Several times, when she was irately questioned by her aunt or governess concerning who she thought she was talking to, she was on the point of answering 'the Thingummyjig': but managed to restrain herself in time. So the secret liaison between them continued unchecked until the day of her eleventh birthday, when her great-grandfather disappeared.

Most of the morning Clarissa had roamed about the garden, partly because a family party was being held for her in the afternoon which meant the old man would be down to meet his relations, and partly because she wanted support, moral or otherwise, from the Thingummyjig.

She hated and was terrified of the approaching party which meant she'd have to be on such good behaviour, she'd inevitably drop something or say the wrong thing when one of the old men addressed her. If she'd had a pretty dress to wear things might have been easier. But Clarissa, despite her name was a plain child, and her aunt considered spending money on such useless vanity as an immoral waste, a fact Clarissa well knew and understood, thanks to the Thingummyjig. Oh yes; the Thingummyjig was very wise. Though he hadn't much voice to speak of ... just a thin high kind of squeak in her ear, he taught her a great deal.

That being the case Clarissa wasn't unduly surprised when the old man disappeared in his wheel chair during the early hours of the afternoon. The Thingummyjig had whispered something was going to happen, so it didn't really shock her at all.

The rest of the household, naturally, was in a panic.

'He was *there* ... sitting in his chair under the elm with his pipe and paper before him, only ten minutes ago...' the aunt said with undisguised hysteria in her voice. 'What could have got into him? He seemed better than usual, more contented, and was *so* looking forward to the party...' her words trailed off into a nervous gasp, before she added, 'There's only one way he could have taken ... down the drive and out of the gates towards the marsh. Someone would have seen him the other side, at the front of the house ... we were all there preparing the tables and seeing the places were properly laid. *You...*' turning to Clarissa, 'did *you* see him move, Clarissa?'

Clarissa shook her head dumbly, eyes and mouth solemn in her pale face. She had a sly conviction the Thingummyjig knew something about it, but as none but her believed in him there was no point in saying so.

Naturally a search party was organised immediately, but it was not until early evening that the old man's body was found, still seated in his invalid chair that had sunk several feet into the dark mud of the marsh, head tipped back just above the oozing water, glassy eyes staring from greenish-grey face, mouth open and filled with slime, beard and hair bedraggled with weed.

A great tragedy, everyone said, resulting from an ancient man's sudden desire to see again the wide expanse of marsh where he'd wandered as a child. The brakes of the chair were intact, there was nothing at all wrong with the mechanics. The kindest verdict therefore was death by misadventure, which was duly recorded.

Shortly afterwards it was decided Clarissa should go to boarding school, which meant naturally a sundering of her childhood relationship with the Thingummyjig.

She told him so the day before she left, and he didn't like it at all. From being a tubby ball of a creature he became suddenly a looming black snake-like thing with vicious red eyes and a fiery tongue darting from his down-drawn elongated mouth.

Clarissa drew back. 'Go away,' she shouted. 'Go away, do you hear? I don't want you...'

She turned and ran into the house, almost knocking her aunt over in the hall.

'*Clarissa.* What's the matter child?' Her thin hand closed in a claw-like grip on the girl's arm. 'Tell me, do you hear ...?'

'The Thingummyjig,' Clarissa blurted out. 'It was ... it was ... well, nothing,' she amended lamely. 'Not anything really. Just...'

'I know. Imagination. You're tired and overwrought, because of going to school.' For the first time Clarissa sensed real concern in her guardian's voice. 'Well, my dear, we've probably kept you too long at home. But with grandfather alive it was difficult ... try and understand. I hadn't the power or money to do as I wished for you. Now it will be more fun. At school you'll make friends in time. *Real* friends of your own age. You'll see.'

Her words proved to be prophetic, although it took a whole term for Clarissa to become adjusted to the new life. And during all that time she did not see the Thingummyjig once.

260

Not even when she returned to the house for holidays, though she knew if she let herself she might easily see him lurking in the shadows or poking from a door. But she didn't. As far as she was concerned the Thingummyjig had disappeared from her life for ever.

Or so she thought.

Following her last term at school she went to university to take her degree in English, with a view to obtaining a teaching post in the future. She was not attractive and considered marriage highly unlikely. Students and tutors accepted her with a certain respect simply because she had undoubted imagination and a capacity to study. Otherwise she went through the usual routine of college life rather like some shy brown bird, unnoticed by more colourful companions. Then, shortly before graduation, she heard that her aunt had died, and as she was the sole heir to the estate, she had to leave immediately for Froggetts.

The late autumn sky was lowering over the marsh when the taxi drew up at the house, spreading an eerie glitter of greenish-black over the desolate flat lands. A solitary wild-fowl, wings outspread, rose squawking into the air from the terrain beyond the garden. There was a seeping chill wind blowing; and the few trees waved black and leafless bordering the front drive.

As she went up the path to the door, there was a drawing of bolts and a shivering glow of light from the hall. The housekeeper stood waiting to receive her, a little more bent, her face thinner and more austere from age, her voice more disapproving as she said, 'So it's yours now, miss. Sad ... very; that the mistress had to go so sudden, I mean.'

'Yes.' Clarissa remarked, putting her case down at the foot of the stairs.

'We've no boy or man now to cart things about,' the woman resumed pointedly, 'and I'm not young any more.'

'Of course not. I can quite well carry it myself,' Clarissa told her.

'Your room's all ready,' the housekeeper continued, still in dull cold tones. 'Your old room. And the mistress is laid out beautifully in the front sitting room. I knew you'd wish it that way ... to see her once before the lid was closed.'

Clarissa shuddered.

'Oh I don't know. I ...'

During the bleak pause she could feel the ancient retainer's eyes boring as though into her very soul.

'Yes, miss?'

Clarissa, intimidated, pulled herself together quickly. 'Naturally. Yes. You're quite right of course.'

But the idea was more than distasteful to her; actually quite horrible. She hated dead things, and ever since her great-grandfather's funeral so many years ago, had been depressed by the very mention of the word. If there had been a way of getting out of her aunt's, she'd have taken it; and it was then she began to think of the Thingummyjig, recalling from the past the lumpy squat shape with the round head, large feet and no legs ... the familiar crony of her childhood who'd possessed such power to help and warn her of approaching crisis. Why had she dismissed him so cruelly on that far off day before being packed off to school? She recalled with shock the writhing violent thing he'd become ... the stretched neck and burning eyes emanating such hatred. Well, no wonder after all he'd done for her.

Poor Thingummyjig.

Later, when she'd gone to bed, following the enforced ordeal of looking down on her aunt's swathed form in its oblong coffin, she tried to pull her mind to normality once more, telling herself over and over again there was *no* Thingummyjig; there never had been, really, it was just ... but *what* was it. At that point her brain boggled, because she knew she was fooling with the truth. In the past only the Thingummyjig had made life for her possible. If *he* hadn't pushed the chair into the marsh on her eleventh birthday she'd never had escaped from Froggetts or gone to school or University, her great-grandfather would have lived on and on, with his awful bangings and threats of punishment ... of ... 'Thrash her, woman. It's discipline she needs, thrash her.'

And she'd had more than she could bear ...
until she'd found the Thingummyjig. Now she
was back again in the beastly house, with the
ugly memories rearing and torturing her
almost to madness.

'Oh Thingummyjig,' she whispered without
realising it, 'Come back, please; forgive me;
help me, Thingummyjig.'

Outside a lean black branch of a tree tapped
at her window, claw-like, resembling the dark
silhouette of a skeleton hand. There was the
moaning of fitful wind from the marsh; a
sighing and creaking through the undergrowth
and huddled bent bushes of the garden as
clouds raced over the face of the moon.

Then she saw it ... pale round visage above a
squat body, with fat fleshy fingers fumbling at
the woodwork where the air blew between
glass and frame, wide mouth extended in an
exultant malicious grin.

She sat up with a lurch of her heart, crying
'Thingummyjig, Thingummyjig,' eyes wide
and staring, arms raised towards him. The
window opened soundlessly, and he was on her
counterpane seated like some midget troll
eyeing her with a strange unholy knowledge.
The giant mahogany wardrobe, old fashioned
dressing table with its archaic ewer and jug,
and looming chest-of-drawers, which a few
moments before had so oppressed her, were
suddenly diminished to no consequence.
'What shall I do, Thingummyjig?' she
whispered.

He slithered off the bed and padded on flat soundless feet to her door, with a curious rolling gait like that of some large ball. When he turned his moon-face towards her his small sloe eyes held a reptilian glitter that told her he'd worked things out. He was hers again to do what she wished at her bidding, so long as *he* wished it too.

He had forgiven her for rejecting him those many years ago.

So she slipped on a pair of light shoes with a dark coat over her nightdress, and followed his slithering form along the landing, down the sombre staircase and through the flagged hall that was in complete darkness, to the front door. She lifted a hand mechanically to the bolts and lock. They gave at her touch with the merest whisper of a grating sound; then she was outside on the drive, running softly after the Thingummyjig, who lolloped and sprang, laughing gleefully but soundlessly through the cold air, turning every few seconds to beckon her on, a childlike, absurd, but incredibly evil looking creature, with a lusting vengeful gleam on his fleshy lascivious face. There was nothing remotely comical about him any more; but in her gratitude at having him there, and faith in his capacity to free her from the haunting dark horror of Froggetts, she didn't notice it.

Not even when they reached the churchyard where her grandfather lay buried.

Then, with a sudden squeal, the loathsome little creature bounced up into the air, landing like a balloon on the black slab of marble, sitting with legless large feet akimbo, grinning impishly in the moonlight close against the upright memorial stone.

As the eerie light fell in a bluish beam across its face, fear slowly spread in a welling wave of terror through Clarissa's numbed mind. Her teeth were chattering as she whispered pleadingly, 'What is it, Thingummyjig, what's the matter?'

The stretched mouth widened further for a moment, before it flickered and died into a grimacing distorted sneer that lengthened and became one with the snaking black neck reaching and quivering above her, eyes mere dots of angry fire, darting tongue spitting and snarling, as a voice ... no longer the Thingummyjig's, but her great-grandfather's voice muttered maliciously, 'Why did you push me into the marsh, Clarissa? That was a very wicked thing to do ...?'

Too terrified to move she watched all that was left of the Thingummyjig merge into the frightful spectral shape of the old man. He was smiling, a ghastly threatening smile, one tooth-fang jutting from the decayed jaws. Green slime dripped from his straggling white hair, he had a skeleton hand outstretched to claim her, as the mournful wind carried the echo of his voice ... 'Naughty girls must be punished

Clarissa ... you know that, don't you ... and it was a *very* wicked thing to kill me ...'

She screamed once. The sound rose more shrill and high than any wild bird's into the damp night air. Then, suddenly, there was a thud as she fell face down on the slab of the old man's tomb.

In the morning she was found by the gardener lying quite dead wearing a dark coat and night attire fallen over her grandfather's grave. There was no indication of why she'd gone there, although the general opinion was that the poor lady had become unhinged by her aunt's death, which must have revived memories of the old man's tragic demise those many years before, inducing a heart attack.

Only one thing puzzled the authorities ... a small scrap of paper in her pocket on which she'd scribbled ... 'Thingummyjig, please help me. I need you ...'

Thingummyjig! What an idea. Obviously grief had shocked the unfortunate creature back into the realms of childhood. The human mind was a queer thing and no mistake. And after all they *had* been a united family at Froggetts.

The housekeeper said nothing. It was not her place. But her opinion was entirely satisfactory to herself. Most people got what they asked for in the end, and Miss Clarissa had certainly deserved her fate.

An unruly child, and a feelingless creature into the bargain.

Nemesis.

That was it.

CHAPTER EIGHTEEN

SITTING TENANT

Sleet was driven on a thin sea-wind against the walls and windows of the old house, filming the skeleton trees outside with a shroud of grey soon turned to the white of thickening snow as evening approached.

In another week it would be Christmas, and in her small flat at the back, old Agatha Treen, daughter of the original owner of the property, moved from her fireside chair to the window, staring wistfully through the blurred air across the valley to the small fishing town huddled below. Lights were already sprinkling the half dark, rekindling her memory vaguely with visions of years long passed, when she had been young and had her family about her ... mother, father, brothers, sisters and a jolly crowd of servants to make the festive season rich and glowing. There had been laughter then, life and warmth and friendliness. Yes: Trengale had been a friendly house, until first one, then another, had left or died.

How long it was since the last of the Treens, her sister Ann had gone, old Agatha couldn't quite remember, but it must have been more than thirty years. Trengale had passed into strangers' hands ... through some muddling business about debts and mortgages she couldn't understand. But they hadn't been able to turn her out. Instead the old family house had been cut up into different sections, and she'd ensconced herself into the two rooms where she still remained, shutting herself away from the constant stream of tenants who moved in for a time, then, for some obscure reason left, saying the premises weren't suitable for families.

Not *suitable*! What a *ridiculous* statement. It had always been for families ... or at least *one* family ... hers. If it hadn't been she wouldn't have stayed herself, putting up with resentment and grumbles, the endless protests that she'd no right there. No right? She had every right, and the knowledge of the continued ill will had hurt her so much during the years, that at last she'd become a hermit and never ventured further than her door, leading into the hall, where she'd peeped out just occasionally to see what was going on. Now she no longer bothered to do that. It was no use. The tenants who came and went had never been friendly, which was a shame. Not that she expected *intimate* overtures from strangers, but a pleasant word now and then would have been helpful, and she was sure the house would have appreciated it too.

A lonely place it seemed these days, and often with a longing for company. Houses after all weren't only bricks and mortar, they were the receptacles of life and history, filled with the memories of those who'd once lived and been there. Memories didn't lie; she knew that. They lingered long after people had gone, filling each corner, each nook and alcove with stories of the past, so that the very air had a life of its own.

She sighed momentarily, a sigh of longing that was caught up by the wind's moan from outside, drifting through each crack of window and floorboards, sending old Agatha back to her chair, where she sat rocking to and fro, thinking, 'Perhaps this time it will be different. These new people, ... they may be happy and kinder; with children perhaps. Christmas is the children's time. It would be nice to have young things about.'

As her thoughts wandered on, one small brown bird, then another, came pecking at the window. She got up and opened it just sufficiently for the feathered creatures to fly inside, muttering, 'Come along then, come along. It's warm in here.'

But was it? She didn't really know any more; cold and warmth had become mingled in a curious way into her mind. There was only one warmth that mattered; life had taught her that ... the warmth of the heart. The warmth these new people should have who were arriving the next day.

She'd almost forgotten. Tomorrow, of course. Tomorrow a fresh family were coming.

She'd listened recently, when that pompous agent had called saying, 'I can assure you sir ... madam, it's a perfectly sound and respectable property, and going for a song, if I may say so. A true bargain for a couple like you, with a family ...'

'But why?' a feminine voice had asked, rather a sweet voice old Agatha had thought, with her ear to her door's crack, '*Why* is it so cheap?'

A cough, a clearing of the throat. Then the silly reply, 'Because of the small back flat, madam. It's got a ...'

A sitting tenant, Miss Treen had thought, moving away. Stupid old thing. What a phrase to use ... as though she spent all her time perched on the sofa or in her rocking chair, when there was so much to do, seeing that everything remained as it was; furniture cared for and nicely polished ... her father's rosewood desk in its place near enough to the window for light, and to the fire for comfort; the pictures steady on the walls, and carpet and floor as clean and clear as she could keep them. The old clock needed repairing, but if the newcomers were kindly people perhaps one of them would go to the village sometime and get old Mr Pert to bring his bag of tools and repair it. Mr Pert was good with his hands; a natural genius, her father had said. But of course that was a long time ago. He might even be dead now.

The thought was saddening. However, whether the clock was going or not was not of primary importance. Her first business was to see that Trengale was at its best to receive company; and for that, she too, had to be ready. Yes, for the first time for many many years, she meant to be dressed in her best clothes, black taffeta with the lace 'bertha' at her shoulders, white froth of a lace cap perched above her sleekly brushed-back hair, her face rosy and shiny from soap and water, a smile on her lips.

'Don't worry, my old darling,' she whispered to the house, 'everything will be handsome for thee tomorrow. There'll be no hard talk of getting me out and leaving you all lonesome. Tomorrow's going to be a real Christmas welcome.' And it seemed to her the walls chuckled with delight.

The next day the snow had thickened and lay everywhere outside in a cloak of soft crusty white. Even the sands bordering the harbour glistened pale and frozen under the lifting morning light. But none was falling any more. All was quiet with the hushed, still quality of nature waking slowly from a timeless dream.

And then, about eleven-thirty, there was the sound of an engine and a car's crunching up the neglected drive. It drew up outside the door, and the silent air was suddenly alive with the chatter and excited echo of human voices.

Old Agatha, her eyes bright in her round

face, as the small birds' fluttering about her kitchen, was already peeping between the narrow crack of her door when they entered, a mother and father obviously, grandparents, a young girl who looked like a help, and five jostling eager children. A family ... a *real* family for once. None of your tight-lipped toffee-nosed couples with a grudge against the place from the beginning ... no thin-faced disagreeable women wanting to poke and pry everywhere, following a first step inside, no high falutin' men demanding a bathroom to every room, or suspicious greedy city dweller wanting to get a hand on her own privacy.

These people, she sensed, were going to be all right. And so was she.

Before they'd got upstairs with their luggage, she was already waiting at the foot of the steps, beaming and bowing, offering all that was in her of friendliness and welcome.

They seemed a little surprised at first, then a small boy said, 'Look mummy, what a nice old lady.'

A strange look passed the mother's face, then she said hesitantly, 'Yes ... and you are ...?'

'Miss Treen,' Agatha told her, with the old realisation that her voice was only a whisper in her own ears. 'Agatha Treen.'

The young woman, though shaken, smiled, 'It's nice to meet you. We've heard quite a lot, of course, but I'm sure we'll all be happy here.'

'And you don't mind?' Agatha's voice by then was no more than a frail sigh through the corridor.

The young head turned slowly from side to side in negation. 'Of course not. Why should we?'

Whether old Agatha really got her next words out, she couldn't tell, as it was just her heart speaking. But the message was unmistakable.

'This house needs love. It's a lonely house, my dears ... and it's Christmas. Care for it, as I have, through the years, and bless you for your understanding.'

The next moment she had turned and gone to her room, caught up into the soft comfort of the waiting shadows.

The following day, curious about the affair, unable to decide quite what had been real and what imagination, the young mother went to the back room, knocked, and receiving no reply, turned the knob.

To her surprise it was unlocked.

She went in, and saw there only an empty room draped by curtains of cobwebs and dust. There was no furniture or sign that it had been lived in for many years. Decades probably. No evidence of life or movement at all but the sudden twitter and flapping of wings, as two or three small brown feathered creatures flew up into the dusty air, circling for a few seconds before taking off through the half open window.

One remained behind, as though loath to leave, perching itself briefly on the warm feminine shoulder, its eyes searching enquiringly for something beyond crumbs or food, something that the young mother realised would remain there now, for always ... human contact, and the knowledge that the sitting tenant had at last found peace.

We hope you have enjoyed this Large Print book. Other Chivers Press or Thorndike Press Large Print books are available at your library or directly from the publishers.

For more information about current and forthcoming titles, please call or write, without obligation, to:

Chivers Press Limited
Windsor Bridge Road
Bath BA2 3AX
England
Tel. (01225) 335336

OR

Thorndike Press
P.O. Box 159
Thorndike, Maine 04986
USA
Tel. (800) 223-2336

All our Large Print titles are designed for easy reading, and all our books are made to last.